P9-CFV-774

Z FOR ZACHARIAH

Z FOR ZACHARIAH

Robert C. O'Brien

Atheneum · 1975 · New York

Library of Congress Cataloging in Publication Data

O'Brien, Robert C.
Z for Zachariah.

SUMMARY: *Seemingly the only person left alive after the holocaust of a war, a young girl is relieved to see a man arrive into her valley until she realizes that he is a tyrant and she must somehow escape.*
I. Title.
PZ7.O135Zaf [Fic] 74-76736
ISBN *0-689-30442-0*

Copyright © 1974 by Sally Conly
All rights reserved
Library of Congress catalog card number 74-76736
ISBN *0-689-30442-0*
Published simultaneously in Canada by
McClelland & Stewart, Ltd.
Manufactured in the United States of America by
Halliday Lithograph Corporation
West Hanover, Massachusetts
First Edition

+
Ob64z

For Jim Cerruti and Bob Jordan

ONE

May 20

I am afraid.

Someone is coming.

That is, I think someone is coming, though I am not sure, and I pray that I am wrong. I went into the church and prayed all this morning. I sprinkled water in front of the altar, and put some flowers on it, violets and dogwood.

But there is smoke. For three days there has been smoke, not like the time before. That time, last year, it rose in a great cloud a long way away, and stayed in the sky for two weeks. A forest fire in the dead woods, and then it rained and the smoke stopped. But this time it is a thin column, like a pole, not very high.

And the column has come three times, each time in the late afternoon. At night I cannot see it, and in the morning it is gone. But each afternoon it comes again, and it is nearer. At first it was behind Claypole Ridge, and I could see only the top of it, the smallest smudge. I thought it was a cloud, except that it was too gray, the wrong color, and then I thought: there are no clouds anywhere else. I got the binoculars and saw that it was narrow and straight; it was smoke from a small fire. When we used to go in the truck, Claypole Ridge was fifteen miles, though it looks closer, and the smoke was coming from behind that.

Beyond Claypole Ridge there is Ogdentown, about ten miles farther. But there is no one left alive in Ogdentown.

I know, because after the war ended, and all the telephones went dead, my father, my brother Joseph and Cousin David went in the truck to find out what was happening, and the first place they went was Ogdentown. They went early in the morning; Joseph and David were really excited, but Father looked serious.

When they came back, it was dark. Mother had been worrying—they took so long—so we were glad to see the truck lights finally coming over Burden Hill, two miles away. They looked like beacons. They were the only lights anywhere, except in the house—no other cars had come down all day. We knew it was the truck because one of the lights, the left one, always blinked when it went over a bump. It came up to the house, and they got out; the boys weren't excited anymore. They looked scared, and my father looked sick. Maybe he was beginning to be sick, but mainly I think he was distressed.

My mother looked up at him as he climbed down.

"What did you find?"

He said: "Bodies. Just dead bodies. They're all dead."

"All?"

We went inside the house where the lamps were lit, the two boys following, not saying anything. My father sat down. "Terrible," he said, and again, "terrible, terrible. We drove around, looking. We blew the horn. Then we went to the church and rang the bell. You can hear it five miles away. We waited two hours, but nobody came. I went in a couple of houses—the Johnsons', the Peters'—they were all in there, all dead. There were dead birds all over the streets."

My brother Joseph began to cry. He was fourteen. I think I had not heard him cry for six years.

May 21

It is coming closer. Today it was almost on top of the ridge, though not quite, because when I looked with the binoculars I could not see the flame, but still only the smoke—rising very fast, not far above the fire. I know where it is: at the crossroads. Just on the other side of

3

the ridge, the east-west highway, the Dean Town Road, crosses our road. It is Route Number 9, a state highway, bigger than our road, which is County Road 793. He has stopped there and is deciding whether to follow Number 9 or come over the ridge. I say *he* because that is what I think of, though it could be *they* or even *she*. But I think it is he. If he decides to follow the highway, he will go away, and everything will be all right again. Why would he come back? But if he comes to the top of the ridge, he is sure to come down here, because he will see the green leaves. On the other side of the ridge, even on the other side of Burden Hill, there are no leaves; everything is dead.

There are some things I need to explain. One is why I am afraid. Another is why I am writing in this composition book, which I got from Klein's store a mile up the road.

I took the book and a supply of ball-point pens back in February. By then the last radio station, a very faint one that I could hear only at night, had stopped broadcasting. It had been dead for about three or four months. I say *about*, and that is one reason I got the book: because I discovered I was forgetting when things happened, and sometimes even *whether* things happened or not. Another reason I got it is that I thought writing in it might be like having someone to talk to, and if I read it back later it would be like someone talking to me. But the truth is I haven't written in it much after all, because

4

there isn't much to write about.

Sometimes I would put in what the weather was like, if there was a storm or something unusual. I put in when I planted the garden because I thought that would be useful to know next year. But most of the time I didn't write, because one day was just like the day before, and sometimes I thought—what's the use of writing anyway, when nobody is ever going to read it? Then I would remind myself: sometime, years from now, *you're* going to read it. I was pretty sure I was the only person left in the world.

But now I have something to write about. I was wrong. I am not the only person left in the world. I am both excited and afraid.

At first when all the others went away, I hated being alone, and I watched the road all day and most of the night hoping that a car, *anybody*, would come over the hill from either direction. When I slept, I would dream that one came and drove on past without knowing I was here; then I would wake up and run to the road looking for the taillight disappearing. Then the weeks went by and the radio stations went off, one by one. When the last one went off and stayed off, it came to me, finally, that nobody, no car, was ever going to come. Of course I thought it was the batteries in my radio that had run down, so I got new batteries from the store. I tried them in the flashlight and it lit, so I knew it was really the station.

Anyway, the man on the last radio station had said he was going to have to go off; there wasn't any more power. He kept repeating his latitude and longitude, though he was not on a ship, he was on land—somewhere near Boston, Massachusetts. He said some other things, too, that I did not like to hear. And that started me thinking. Suppose a car came over the hill, and I ran out, and whoever was in it got out—suppose he was crazy? Or suppose it was someone mean, or even cruel, and brutal? A murderer? What could I do? The fact is, the man on the radio, toward the end, sounded crazy. He was afraid; there were only a few people left where he was and not much food. He said that men should act with dignity even in the face of death, that no one was better off than any other. He pleaded on the radio, and I knew something terrible was happening there. Once he broke down and cried on the radio.

So I decided: if anyone does come, I want to see who it is before I show myself. It is one thing to hope for someone to come when things are civilized, when there are other people around, too. But when there is nobody else, then the whole idea changes. This is what I gradually realized. There are worse things than being alone. It was after I thought about that, that I began moving my things to the cave.

May 22

The smoke came again this afternoon, still in the same place as yesterday. I know what he (*she? they?*) is

6

doing. He came down from the north. Now he is camping in that spot, at the crossroads, and exploring east and west on Number 9, the Dean Town Road. That worries me. If he explores east and west he is sure to explore south, too.

It also lets me know some things. He is sure to be carrying some fairly heavy supplies and equipment. He leaves these at the crossroads while he makes side trips, so he can go faster. It also means he probably hasn't seen anyone else along the way, wherever he came from, or he wouldn't leave his stuff. Or else he has somebody with him. Of course he could be just resting. He might have a car, but I doubt that. My father said that cars would stay radioactive for a long time—because they're made of heavy metal, I suppose. My father knew quite a lot about things like that. He wasn't a scientist, but he read all the scientific articles in the newspapers and magazines. I suppose that's why he got so worried after the war ended when all the telephones went off.

The day after they took the trip to Ogdentown, they went again. This time they went with two cars, our truck and Mr. Klein's, the man who owned the store. They thought that was better, in case one broke down; Mr. Klein and his wife went, too, and finally Mother decided to go. I think she was afraid of being separated from my father; she was more worried than ever after she heard what happened in Ogdentown. Joseph was to stay at home with me.

This time they were going south, first through the gap

7

to where the Amish lived to see how they had come through the bombing. (Not that they had been bombed —the nearest bombs had been a long way off; Father thought a hundred miles or more; we could hardly hear the rumble, though we felt the earth shake.) The Amish farms were just south of our valley. The Amish were friends of ours and especially of Mr. Klein's, being the main customers at his store. Since they had no cars but only horses and wagons they did not often drive all the way to Ogdentown.

Then, after they saw the Amish they were going to circle west and join the highway to Dean Town, passing through Baylor on the way. Dean Town is a real city— twenty thousand people, much bigger than Ogdentown. It was to Dean Town I was supposed to go year after next, to the Teachers' College. I am hoping to be an English teacher.

They started out early in the morning, Mr. Klein leading the way in his panel truck. My father put his hand on my head when they left, the way he used to when I was six years old. David said nothing. They had been gone about an hour when I discovered that Joseph was nowhere to be found, and I figured out where he was: hidden in the back of Mr. Klein's truck. I should have thought of that. We were both afraid of being left behind, but my father said we should stay, to water the animals and to be here in case somebody came, or in case they got the telephones going again and ours should ring. Well, it never rang, and nobody came.

My family never came back, and neither did Mr. and Mrs. Klein. I know now there weren't any Amish, nor anybody in Dean Town. They were all dead, too.

Since then I have climbed the hills on all sides of this valley, and at the top I have climbed a tree. When I look beyond, I see that all the trees are dead, and there is never a sign of anything moving. I don't go out there.

TWO

May 23

I am writing this in the morning, about 10:30, while I rest after doing some things I had to do. I didn't want to, but if I had waited until he came over the ridge, and then over Burden Hill where I could see him—where my valley begins—it would have been too late.

These are the things I had to do:

Let the chickens out of the chicken yard. I chased them out. They are all free now. I can catch them again later, or most of them, if they aren't out too long.

Let the two cows and the calf, the young bull calf, out through the pasture gate. I had to chase them, too. They will be all right for a while. There is still good grass in the far fields down the road, water in the pond, and the calf will keep the fresh cow milked. They are Guernseys. Generally I have had good luck with the animals, and taken good care of them. The chickens have kept on laying, and there are two more now than there were at the beginning. Only the dog, David's dog, Faro, ran off. He just wasn't there one morning, and he never came back. I suppose he went out of the valley, looking for David, and died.

Dig up the vegetable garden, everything that was coming up, flatten it, and cover it with dead leaves. It does not show at all. I hated that the worst, because everything was growing so well. But I have enough canned and dried stuff to live on; and if he had seen the garden, all in rows and weeded, he would have known someone was here.

I am sitting at the entrance to the cave. From here I can see most of the valley, my own house and barn, the roof of the store, the little steeple on the old church (some of the boards are off the side—can I fix them? I don't know), and part of the brook that runs by about fifty feet away. And I can see the road where it comes over Burden Hill, and almost to where it disappears again through the pass—about four miles altogether. But I do not think he will see the cave, since it is halfway up the hillside behind the house, and the trees hide the opening, which is small. Joseph, David, and I did not find it for years, and we played near it every day, or nearly.

He will find the house of course, the store and the church, but he must have found a lot of those on his way. By luck I have not dusted the house recently. This morning I looked at it carefully, and I do not think there are any signs that I have been in it recently. I took the flowers off the altar in the church. I brought the two lamps up here, and a supply of oil.

Now I will wait. I said it was about 10:30, but I'm not really sure of the time. My wristwatch runs all right, but I have nothing to set it by except the sun. I'm not really even sure of the date. I have a calendar, but it is hard—really hard—to keep track even so. At first I would check off each day with a pencil. Then, later in the day, I would see the calendar and start thinking: did I check today or didn't I? The more I thought, the more I couldn't remember. I'm pretty sure I missed some days, and other times I may have checked two. Now I have a better system; I have an alarm clock I set; I keep it right on the calendar, and when it goes off I check the day. I do this only in the morning; in the evening I wind and reset the clock.

I think I know how to be sure of the date soon. I have a *Farmer's Almanack* that tells the longest day of the year, June 22. So in a few weeks I will try timing the sunrise and sunset each day. Whichever day is longest I will know is June 22.

It isn't really important, I suppose. Except that my

birthday comes on June 15 and I would like to know when it's my birthday and keep track of how old I am. I will be sixteen on my next one, about three weeks from now.

I could write a lot about things like that—things I had to figure out when I first realized that I was alone and going to be alone, maybe for the rest of my life. The luckiest thing was that the store was there, and that it was a big store, a general store, well stocked because of the Amish trade. Another lucky thing was that the war ended in the spring (it began in the spring, too, of course—it only lasted a week), so that I had all summer to understand how things were, to get over being afraid, and to think about how I was going to live through the winter.

Heat, for instance. The house had an oil furnace and a gas stove. When the telephone went off, so did the electricity, and the furnace wouldn't run without electricity. The gas stove would work, but it used bottled gas; I knew that the tanks (there are two) would run out eventually, and when they did, the gas truck would not come to replace them. But the house has two fireplaces, one in the living room, one in the dining room, and there was about a cord of wood in the woodshed, already cut. Still I knew that wouldn't be enough, so that was how I spent quite a few mornings in the spring, summer, and fall—cutting wood with a bucksaw (I got a new one from the store, one of the tubular kind) and hauling it in the old hand truck that was stored in the barn. By closing off the rest of the house I kept those two rooms warm enough—really warm, except for a couple of very cold days. Then I just wore some extra sweaters. By being careful with the gas, I made it last most of the winter; then I cooked on the fireplace, which is a lot of trouble because it gets the pans so dirty. There is an old wood-coal stove in the barn that my mother used to use before we got gas. This summer I'm going to try—that is, I *was* going to try—to haul it to the house. It's heavier than I can lift, but I think I can take it apart. I've already put oil on all the bolts to loosen them.

I started this in the morning, while I was resting. Then I did some more work, ate some lunch, and now it is afternoon.

The smoke has come again. It is definitely on this side of Claypole Ridge. As nearly as I can guess, about halfway between the ridge and Burden Hill. That means he (*they? she?*) has seen the valley and is on his way to it.

I feel as if it is the beginning of the end. I must make up my mind what to do.

A strange thing. Whoever it is, he is certainly moving slowly. If he came over the ridge, as he had to do, he must have seen the valley and the green trees, because the ridge is higher than Burden Hill. You can see the valley from there, I know—the far end of it at least—

because I've done it so many times myself. So you'd think he would be in a hurry. If he walked toward Dean Town, or the other way, east on Number 9, he saw only the deadness, as I have seen it looking out, everything gray and brown and all the trees like stalks. He has probably seen nothing else all the way, wherever he came from. And between the ridge and Burden Hill he is still in it. The distance is only about eight miles—yet he seems to have stopped halfway and camped.

Tomorrow morning I may go up near the top of Burden Hill, climb a tree and watch. I won't go on the road. There is a path that goes in the same direction but is in the woods higher up the hillside. In fact the woods has quite a lot of paths. I know them all. If I go, I will take one of my guns, the light one, the .22 rifle. I am a good shot with that, better than Joseph or David, though I have only practiced on cans and bottles. The big one, Father's deer rifle, has too much kick. I have shot it, but I tend to wince when I pull the trigger, and that throws my aim off. I don't expect to use the gun anyway, really, I don't like guns. I just think I ought to have it along. After all, I don't know what to expect.

Tonight I have to get some more water into the cave and to cook some stuff. I won't be able to build a fire after he reaches the valley. By day he would see the smoke, at night he would see the flame because it has to be outside. We built a fire in the cave once and had to run outside because the smoke got so thick. Tonight I will cook some chicken, boil some eggs (hard), and make some cornmeal bread, so I won't have to eat just canned things, at least for a while.

I could get water by sneaking to the brook at night. But I think it is safer to store some. I have six big bottles—cider jugs—with tops.

That was another thing I had to decide about when the electricity went off: water. There was—there is—a drilled well near the house, about sixty feet deep, with an electric pump. We had an electric hot water heater, a shower, tub, all that; but of course they all stopped working. It happened before my family left. So we had to carry water. You can't lower a bucket into a drilled well; the hole is too small, so that left us a choice of two brooks. The one that flows past the cave, the one I can see from here, goes on down toward the house but then turns left into the pasture, where it widens into a good pond—a small lake, really, clear and quite deep, with bream and bass in it. The other, named Burden Creek (after my family, like the hill—the Burdens were the first to settle in this valley), is bigger and wider, also nearer to the house. It flows more or less parallel to the road, and out of the valley through the gap at the south. It is really a small river, and quite beautiful, or used to be.

Since it was nearer, we thought we would carry water to the house from that—two buckets at a time as needed. Then, just in time, Joseph and I, who went down the first time, noticed something. It had fish in it, too, though not as big or as many as the pond. But that first time we went to get water we saw a dead fish floating past. I found a dead turtle on the bank. This stream flows into the valley out of a sort of cleft in the rock ridge to the left of Burden Hill—the water comes from outside, and it was poisoned. We looked a long time (we kept back from it, though) and we saw that there was nothing left alive in it at all, not even a frog or a water bug.

We were scared. We ran (with the buckets) all the way to the pond, up to the far end where the small stream flows in. I was never so glad to see a bunch of minnows in my life! They scooted away, just as they always had. The water was all right, and still is. It rises from a spring up the hill, inside the valley, and it must come from deep underground. I catch fish in the pond all the time, and eat them; they have been one of my best food supplies except in the middle of winter, when they stopped biting.

I think I will definitely go in the morning, as soon as it is light. Now that I have decided, I am beginning to worry about something that I know is really foolish: how I look, how I'm dressed. I thought about it this morning when I was at the house, and I looked in the mirror, which I don't often do anymore. I have on blue jeans, but they are men's blue jeans (there are cartons of them at the store, but no girls') so they don't fit too well, but are rather baggy. And a man's work shirt, cotton flannel, and boys' tennis shoes. Not exactly elegant, and my hair isn't exactly stylish—I just cut it off square around my neck. For a while I used to curl it every night—the way I did for school—but that took time, and finally I realized that no one would see it besides me. So it is straight but clean and has turned much lighter because I am outdoors so much. I think I am not as skinny as I used to be, though it is hard to tell in these clothes.

But what I wonder—should I wear a dress? Suppose it *is* a real rescue party, an official group of some kind? I guess I could sneak back and change. I do have one pair of real slacks left. The others wore out. But I haven't had on a dress since the war. Anyway, I can't climb a tree very well in a skirt. But I think I will compromise and wear the good slacks.

May 24

It is a man, one man alone.

This morning I went as I planned. I put on my good slacks, took the .22 and hung the binoculars around my neck. I climbed a tree and saw him coming up the road. I could not really see what he looks like, because he is dressed, entirely covered, in a sort of greenish plastic-looking suit. It even covers his head, and there is a glass mask for his eyes—like the wet suits skin divers wear in cold water, only looser and bulkier. Like skin divers, too, he has an air tank on his back. But I could tell it was a man, even though I could not see his face, by his size and the way he moves.

The reason he is coming so slowly is that he is pulling a wagon, a thing about the size of a big trunk mounted on two bicycle wheels. It is covered with the same green plastic as his suit. It is heavy, and he was having a hard time pulling it up Burden Hill. He stopped to rest every few minutes. He still has about a mile to go to reach the top.

I have to decide what to do.

THREE

Now it is night.

He is in my house.

Or possibly not in it, but just outside it, in a small plastic tent he put up. I cannot be sure, because it is too dark to see clearly. I am watching from the cave, but the fire he built—outside the house, in the yard—has burned down. He built it with my wood.

He came over the top of Burden Hill this afternoon. I was back up to watch, having eaten some lunch and changed back to my blue jeans. I decided not to show myself. I can always change my mind later.

I wondered what he would do when he reached the top. He must have been pretty sure, but not quite, that he was coming to a place where things were living. As I said, you can see the green from the ridge, but not too well—it is a long way. And maybe he has been fooled sometimes; maybe he thought it was a mirage. There is a flat place where the road first reaches the top of the hill—a stretch of about a hundred yards or so before it starts descending again, into the valley. When you get just past the middle of this you can see it all, the river, the house, the barn, the trees, pasture, everything. It was my favorite sight when I had been away, maybe because when I saw it I was always coming home. As it's spring, today it is all a new fresh green.

When he got to that place he stopped. He dropped the shaft of the wagon and just stared for about a minute. Then he ran forward down the road, very clumsy in his plastic suit, waving his arms. He ran to a tree by the roadside and pulled a branch, tearing off the leaves and holding them close to his glass face mask. You could tell he was thinking: Are they real?

I was watching from a place only a little way up the hillside, a path in the woods. I had my gun beside me. I did not know whether he could hear or not with that mask on, but I did not move or make a sound.

All at once he pulled at the mask, at a fastening at the neck of it, as if he were going to take it off. So far I had not been able to see his face at all, but only the glass plate, so I was staring. Then he stopped, and instead ran back to the wagon. He unsnapped the plastic cover from one end of the trunk and pulled it open. He reached inside and took out a glass thing—a sort of tube with a metal rod in it, like a big thermometer. It had some kind of a dial or gauge on it to read—I couldn't see from where I was, but he held it in front of his mask and turned it slowly, studying it. He walked back down the road to the tree, looking at the rod. He held it down close to the blacktop, then up high in the air. Then back to the wagon again.

He took out another machine, something like the first one but bigger; after that he pulled out a black, round thing: it was an earphone, with a wire dangling from it. He plugged the wire into the machine and put the earphone up beside his mask, next to his ear. I could tell what he was doing: using one machine to check against the other. And I knew what they must be; I had read about them but never seen one: radiation counters, Geiger counters they call them. He walked down the road, a long way this time—half a mile at least, watching one counter, listening to the other.

Then he took off the mask and shouted.

It startled me so that I jumped back. I started to run—then I stopped. He was not shouting at me. He was cheering—a long *"Haaay"* sound, the kind they make at football games. He didn't hear me (luckily). The shout went echoing down the valley, and I stood absolutely still again, though my heart was still thumping—it was so long since I had heard any voice except my own, when I sing sometimes.

He was answered by silence. So he put his hands beside his mouth and shouted again, aiming down the hill. This time he called, very loud:

"Anybody here?"

It echoed again. When it stopped, it was strange how much quieter it seemed than before. You get so used to silence you don't notice it. But the sound of his voice was nice, a strong sound. For a minute I almost changed my mind. It came on me in a rush, very strong. I wanted to run down the hill through the woods and call, "I'm here." I wanted to cry, and touch his face. But I caught myself in time, and stayed quiet. He turned, and I looked through my binoculars watching him. He was walking back to the wagon, with his mask hanging down his back like a hood.

He had a beard, and his hair was long and dark brown. What I noticed most, though, was that he was extremely pale. I have gotten used to the tan color of my own hands and arms, but I have seen pictures of coal miners who work all day underground. He looked like that. His face, as well as I could see it, was narrow and long, with quite a big nose. With the long hair, the beard, and the pale white color he looked quite wild, but also, I have to admit, rather poetic. And not very healthy.

He came back to the wagon, looking over his shoulder

a lot, in the direction of my house. I supposed he was thinking: there might be someone there, they could hardly hear from here. He was right. It is nearly a mile from the hilltop to the house. He put one of the machines back into the truck and then he did a surprising thing. He took out a gun and laid it on top of the plastic cover as if he wanted it handy. He kept the other counter out, too, the one with the earphone. Finally he picked up the shaft of the wagon and started down the hill. When the slope got steep he turned the wagon around, so it went ahead and he was pulling back on it. Every fifty feet or so he would turn it sideways, stop, and listen to the earphone. Twice more, too, he called.

Moving as slowly as he did, it was about five o'clock (by my watch) before he reached the bottom of the hill, and dusk before he got to the house. I went back along the high path to the cave, where I am now, and watched him through the binoculars.

When he got to the house, he put down the wagon shaft in the front yard. I am glad now that I did not have time to mow it—I decided last summer that I wouldn't even try, so the grass is knee-high and a lot of weeds have sprung up. Then he began to act in a strange way, to move with great caution. Instead of going to the door, he walked around the house and looked in every window. He stayed back as if he were afraid or did not want to be seen. Finally he went to the door and called again, the same words as before:

"Anybody here?"

This time he said it more quietly, as if he knew somehow that he was not going to get an answer; he had been through it before. Without knocking, he opened the door and went in. Then *I* was nervous. Had I left anything? A half-bucket of fresh water? An egg on the shelf? A lot of things went through my head. Any one of them would give me away. But I didn't think I had.

About twenty minutes later he came out, looking a little bit puzzled. He stood in front of the doorway, staring at the road, thinking. He started toward it, and then apparently changed his mind. I think he was considering going on to the church and the store. You can't see them from the house, but he had seen them both, of course, from the top of the hill; so he knew about where they were. Anyway, he looked at the sky instead; the sun had set and it was getting dark, so he came back to his wagon and opened its plastic cover. This time he pulled several things from it, including a bulky square, which he unfolded and set up—the tent.

He had obviously looked out the kitchen window and seen the woodshed, because when the tent was ready he walked around the house and got some wood to build his fire. After he got it going, he took some more stuff from the wagon. I could not see very well by the firelight—it had grown completely dark—but I could tell he was cooking a meal of some kind. When he had eaten, he sat by the fire for a long time while it slowly died down.

Then, as I said, I couldn't see much but I think he got into the tent. Now I think he is asleep. He could have slept in the house, but I suppose he didn't trust it. I think that green plastic stuff—the suit, the tent, the wagon cover—is something that stops radiation.

I will go in the cave now and sleep. I am still afraid. And yet it is—what is the word I mean?—*companionable* to know there is someone else in the valley.

May 25

It may be that he has made a mistake. I am not sure. And if it was a mistake, I don't know how bad. It worries me, because I suppose I could have stopped him, though I don't know how. Not without showing myself.

When I came out of the cave this morning, very carefully, on hands and knees, keeping my head down, he was already awake, though the sun was barely up. He was folding his tent; he put it back in the wagon, and then several things happened very quickly.

First, somewhere out behind the chicken yard one of the hens cackled. It had laid an egg, of course. Almost immediately a rooster crowed. And from the distance, as if it were answering, one of the cows *mooed*, a real bellow, long and loud. He dropped a pan he was holding and jumped up, listening. He looked amazed, as if he could not believe it. He probably had not heard an animal sound for more than a year.

He stood there for a minute, just listening, staring, and

thinking. After that he got quite busy. He pulled out his radiation counter again—the small one—and looked at it. He was still wearing his plastic suit, though without the helmet. Now he pulled at some kind of fastening on the cuffs, and removed the glove parts that had covered his hands. He reached farther into his wagon-trunk and took out another gun, a big one. It looked like an army gun, a carbine I think, with a square magazine sticking out of the bottom. He looked at it but put it back, and got the smaller gun from the tent. The other was a .22 like mine, only bolt-action, and mine is a pump. He carried it toward the chicken yard.

The chickens weren't in the chicken yard, of course, because I had shut the gate when I chased them out. But some of them, at least, had stayed around it—I knew they would, because that's where I feed them. I couldn't see him back there, because there are some big bushes (lilac and forsythia) between the house and the fence. But in a minute I heard the rifle crack, and a couple of minutes after that he came back carrying a dead chicken. One of *my* chickens!

I could hardly blame him, of course. I don't know what kind of food he carries in that wagon, but whatever it is, I'm sure there is no fresh meat, or fresh anything. So I can understand how the thought of a chicken would make him hungry. (In a few days, I expect, I'll be feeling the same way.) But shooting is not the accepted method of killing a tame chicken. I eat them myself, as we always did, and I have not yet fired a shot from any of my guns, not once since before the war.

He put the chicken down on top of the wagon, and then, without waiting to pluck or clean it, started out immediately down the road in the direction of the church and the store—and the cows. He took the smaller rifle with him; also the glass tube.

For this first day, at least, I thought I had better keep him in sight as much as I could—until I get to know something about his habits. So again I went along a path I know in the woods, about two-thirds of the way up the hillside. That way I could watch him closer up, better than from the cave, where the road disappears for stretches when trees grow near it. I took my binoculars and my own rifle.

He saw the cows right away, as soon as he got past the barn and the fence. They were off by the pond, in the far field. My father used to grow oats there, but luckily that last spring he had rotated it to fescue. They were grazing there quietly, with the calf between them; they were not fenced in, but as I had thought they would, they had stayed near home. When he moved toward them, a stranger, they ran off, though not very far. Cows can tell people apart all right, though it's true they don't care much.

He started to follow them, then changed his mind and walked to the edge of the pond. He stared into the water, first from a few feet away, then, obviously very

interested, kneeling down with his face close to the surface. I could tell he was looking at the minnows—there
are always some up near the edge. He took his glass
counter and held it close to the water; finally he stuck
one end of it *in* the water. He put out his hand, cupped
some and tasted it. It tastes fine; I know, I drink it all the
time, though I get it from the brook at the other end. I
could tell he felt like cheering.

He went on. To the church, where he stayed a few
minutes. To the store, where he stayed much longer. I
couldn't tell what he did inside—examine what was
there, I suppose, and check it with his counter. When he
came out he was carrying a box of something, canned
stuff I thought. That's as far as he walked; from the
store he headed back toward the house. With the box,
the rifle, and the counter he was quite heavily loaded.

Once, on the way, he suddenly put the box down,
raised the rifle and fired into some bushes by the edge of
the road. He probably saw a rabbit. There are quite a
few in the valley; also squirrels, and a few crows who
seem to have had the sense to stay around. The other
birds, moving about as they do, flew out into the deadness and died. Apparently he missed the rabbit.

It was now nearly eleven o'clock; the sun was high
and bright, and the day had turned warm. Wearing that
plastic suit and carrying all that stuff, I could tell he was
getting too hot; he stopped twice to rest and put the
carton down. And that was why, when he got back to

the house, he made the mistake. He went swimming and took a bath in the dead stream, Burden Creek.

First he put the carton down on top of the wagon and took things out of it. As I had guessed, most of it was canned food. But he also took out a couple of bars of soap—I recognized the blue wrappers. Next, to my astonishment, he took off the plastic suit. He simply unzipped it down the front, pulled it down over his legs and stepped out of it. Underneath he was wearing what looked like a very thin, lightweight blue coverall. Down the back and arms it was soaked with sweat.

After that, having been so cautious up till then, he was careless. I can see how he did it. He thought, not knowing the geography of the valley very well, that it was all the same stream. He did not know that there were two streams, and he had seen the fish. Being so hot—and, maybe, not having had a bath in a long time—he picked up the soap and ran across the road. There he took off the coverall and jumped in with a splash. If he had been a little less eager, he might have noticed that there were no fish there, and that all the grass and weeds were dead for about two feet back along both the banks. Quite a few of the trees along the creek are dying, too. But he didn't look. He stayed in quite a long time with his piece of soap.

I said I don't know how bad a mistake it was. That's because I don't know what is wrong with that water. The stream merges with the other one, the pond stream, farther down the valley, and they flow out the gap as one. Downstream from where they merge, they are both dead—I have looked many times, thinking that maybe, after all this time, the water in Burden Creek might be all right again. But no fish swims into it, or if it does, it dies and drifts away.

It might be that if he had taken his glass rod, he would have found the water is radioactive. But I can't be sure. On the radio, at the end of the war, they said the enemy was using nerve gas, bacteria, and "other antipersonnel weapons." So it could be anything. All I can do is wait and watch. I hope it doesn't kill him.

FOUR

It is night again, and I am in the cave with one lamp lit.

An inexplicable thing: the dog, Faro, has come back. How that is possible I don't know. Where has he been? How has he lived? He looks terrible—as thin as a skeleton, and half the hair is gone from his left side.

I think I already wrote that Faro was David's dog. He came with David when David moved in with us, about five years ago after his father died and he became an orphan (his mother died when he was born). Joseph and David were within six months of the same age, so they became really close friends—all three of us were, in fact. But Faro was always really David's dog; he would never go with any of us unless David went, too. He was—he is—a mongrel, but mostly setter, and he loved to hunt. When we went hunting, when he even saw a gun come out, he would get so excited you would never believe he would freeze on a point, but he always did; he was really good. So when David left with my father and mother, and then later the dog disappeared, I assumed he had gone looking for David, through the gap into the deadness. (He used to follow the truck sometimes if David went in it; you had to tie him up.) But apparently he did not go through the gap. He must have been living in the woods up near there, waiting for David to come, eating what he could catch.

I suppose he heard the two gunshots, and that's what brought him back. I was watching at the time. It was about 1:30 and the man, wearing his blue coverall—he did not put the plastic suit back on—had cleaned the chicken with a knife from his wagon and was cooking it on a spit he had made. The dog came up very cautiously and stood at the edge of the front yard, watching and sniffing. When the man looked up and saw him, he stopped turning the spit and stared, not moving. Then he took a step toward Faro, and Faro backed away. The man crouched down, slapped his knee, whistled, and said something; I could hear the whistle but not the words. I knew he was calling Faro, though; he wanted to make friends. He walked forward again, and Faro backed away, keeping the same distance between them.

The man gave up and went back to the fire. That is, he seemed to have given up, but he really had not, I could tell. He had an idea, a very simple one, and he kept looking up to see if the dog was still there. When the chicken was cooked, just a few minutes later, he went into the house and came out with two plates (mine!). He cut off a big chunk of chicken and opened a can from the store-box, some kind of meat. He put the chicken and some of the meat on one plate and carried it, moving very gently, over past the edge of the yard to about where the dog had first appeared. And he put it down there.

Back to his spit he went, very unconcerned, and carved up his chicken and ate it, along with some kind of dried bread (hardtack?) he took from his wagon. (I could have given him some fresh-baked corn bread.) He ate the whole chicken, very quickly too, and as he ate he watched the dog from the corner of his eye. Faro crept up on the food, looking at the man, then the plate of food, then the man again, until finally he reached it. Standing as far back as he could, he stretched out his neck, snatched the chicken and ran back fifty feet. He swallowed it in two gulps, came back for the other meat, and snatched it the same way.

Having eaten, the dog came back to the plate, licked it, and then slowly began circling the yard, sniffing as he went, still keeping away from the man. He went all the way around the house twice. Then, to my horror, he started wagging his tail the way he used to when he was tracking, and he turned from the house and headed up the hill toward the cave. He had found my tracks.

The man stared after him as he left, whistled loudly, and started to follow. But the dog was quickly out of sight, and the man gave up after a few steps. Fortunately the area between the house and the cave has a lot of trees and underbrush, so I am quite sure he got no glimpse of the dog once he'd lost him. I crept back into the cave, and in two minutes Faro came bounding in.

Poor dog. He looked terrible, even worse close up than through the binoculars. He gave two short, creaky little barks and ran to me. But I was scared. Inevitably, if he stayed around, he was going to betray me. So I did not know what to do; I did not dare act too friendly. I said in a whisper, "*Good* Faro," but I did not hug him the way I felt like doing. The truth is, though I liked him and he liked me, it was not me he was looking for. He had been in the cave a thousand times before when we played there, and now he ran around it sniffing everything, looking for David. When he did not find him he left again in just a few minutes and ran back down the hill, toward the house.

That means trouble, because that's where the man is, and the plate, and the food. If the man makes friends with Faro, he will come to a whistle, as he did for David;

the man can keep him close, and follow him when he comes up here.

I suppose it seems wrong to be so afraid of that. But I don't know what the man will do. I liked most people. I had a lot of friends at school. But that was a matter of choice; there were some people I didn't like, and many that I didn't even know. This man may be the only man left on the earth. I don't know him. Suppose I don't like him? Or worse, suppose he doesn't like me?

For nearly a year I have been here alone. I have hoped and prayed for someone to come, someone to talk to, to work with and plan for the future of the valley. I dreamed that it would be a man, for then, some time in the future—it is a dream, I know—there might be children in the valley. Yet, now that a man has actually come, I realize that my hopes were too simple. All men are different. The man on the radio station, fighting to survive, saw people that were desperate and selfish. This man is a stranger, and bigger and stronger than I am. If he is kind, then I am all right. But if he is not—what then? He can do whatever he likes, and I will be a slave for the rest of my life. That is why I want to find out, at least as well as I can by watching, what he is like.

After the dog left the cave, I went back to the entrance and looked down at the house. The man had scissors in his hand, a small mirror propped in front of him, and was cutting his hair and his beard. He kept at it for a long time and trimmed them both quite short. I must admit it made a great improvement; he looks almost handsome, though he got the hair rather lopsided in back, where he could not see it in the mirror.

May 26

A sunny day, like yesterday, only warmer. According to my calendar (I have it and the alarm clock here in the cave) it is Sunday. Ordinarily that would mean I would go to the church in the morning, and try to make the rest of the day a day of rest. Sometimes I would go fishing, a practical way of resting. I would take the Bible with me to the church, and some flowers for the altar in spring and summer. I did not pretend to have any real service, of course, but I would sit and read something from the Bible. Sometimes I chose—I like the Psalms and Ecclesiastes—and sometimes I just opened it at random. In the middle of winter I usually did not go; there was no heat and it was too cold to sit there.

There never were any real services in the church, not in our time, anyway, nor any minister. It is very small, and was built a long time ago by some of our ancestors—"an early Burden," my father used to say—when they first settled in the valley and I guess thought there would be a village here. There never was, since for years afterward there was no road in, just a trail. The road ended past Ogdentown at the junction. When we went to church we drove to Ogdentown.

This morning I had to forget all that. The man got up early and cooked his breakfast, still on a fire out in front of the house; he was quick and purposeful. He obviously had plans and I soon learned what they were: he wanted to explore the length of the valley and take a look beyond. He still did not know how far the green part extended.

Before he went, he put some more of the canned meat in Faro's plate and set it out. Faro himself was nowhere to be seen—at that moment, but as soon as the man started up the road he emerged from the woodshed where he had been sleeping, ate the food, and then followed. You could tell he wanted to join the man—he was carrying the small gun—but could not quite get up his nerve. After a hundred yards or so he turned back, sniffed the plate again, and lay down not far from the tent.

I followed the man, staying on my high woods path. Sooner or later he will explore up here, too, and then I will have to cross to the other side of the valley—also, I will really have to be alert, because in the woods he will not be so visible.

But today he stayed on the road. He did not wear the plastic suit and walked much more briskly without it, so I had to work a bit to keep up with him—the path is not as straight as the road; also I had to be careful not to make noise.

When he got to the store, he went in, and when he came out I was amazed—I hardly recognized him. The wrinkled coverall was gone; he was dressed in a whole new outfit; khaki drill slacks, very neat; a blue work shirt; even new work shoes and a straw cap. (*My* clothes.) He really looked like a different person, and quite nice. For one thing, with his hair and beard trimmed and now neatly dressed, he looked a lot younger, though still much older than I. I would guess maybe thirty or thirty-two.

He walked on down the road, heading south toward the far end of the valley, toward the gap. He looked around him as he went, curious about everything, but he did not slow down much until he reached the culvert. At that point the small stream, having flowed into the pond and out again and meandered along through the meadow, runs into a rise (the beginning of the end of the valley, I suppose), bears right and is joined by Burden Creek.

He stopped there. I think it dawned on him then for the first time that there were two streams, and that the pond was not formed by Burden Creek. And there, if you look closely, the difference between the two becomes plain. I have seen it many times. Even in the last few feet the small stream has life in it—minnows, tadpoles, water bugs (skippers), and green moss on the rocks. Burden Creek has none at all, and after they merge, downstream all the way to the gap and out, the water is clear and dead.

I cannot be sure that he noticed all that, but he stared at the water for a long time, getting down on his hands and knees. If he did see the deadness, he must have begun worrying, and maybe it was then that he started feeling sick. In a short time he was going to be very sick.

However, worried or not, he got up in a few minutes and walked on, striding as briskly as before. In another fifteen minutes he was approaching the end of the valley, and the beginning of the deadness beyond. The road there leads through the gap and on to the Amish farms beyond.

He could not see that, of course. In fact, unless you know, it is hard to believe that there is any way out of the valley at the south end. The gap is in the shape of a very large S, and until you are right on top of it you think you are coming to a solid wall of rock and trees. Then the road (and the stream beside it) turns sharply right, left, and right again, cutting through the ridge like a tunnel without even going uphill.

With Burden Hill on the other end, the result is that the valley is completely closed in. People used to say it even has its own weather; the winds from outside do not blow through it.

When he reached the gap, I lost sight of him—there is no way you can see into it from the hillside where I was. But the stretch of road going through it is only a couple of hundred yards long, so I knew he would reappear shortly. When he saw the dead land outside, he would turn and come back; he could not go farther without his plastic suit.

I sat down in the sun to wait and looked at the scenery below me: the narrow black road running straight and the river winding beside it; the other side of the valley, here quite close, rising gently in woods; big oak and beech trees, old ones with black shadows beneath their branches. Higher up there was a big outcropping of gray rock, a cliff. We used to climb it; it is not as steep as it looks from a distance. It was about eleven o'clock and had turned quite warm. Behind me some blackberry bushes gave off a sweet smell, and there were bees humming in the blossoms. At times like that I miss the songbirds.

He must have stood a while near the end of the gap, resting or looking, because it was twenty minutes before he came out, walking somewhat more slowly, and started toward the house.

About halfway back it happened: he stopped, sat down quickly in the middle of the road, and was very sick to his stomach. He stayed there, retching, leaning to his side on one arm, for several minutes. Then he got up and walked on.

He did this again three times on the way, and after the third time he was barely stumbling along, dragging the rifle. When he reached the tent, he crawled in; he has not come out again. Faro came out eventually, braver

41

now, and sniffed at the opening of the tent. He even wagged his tail a little, and then went and sat by the empty plate.

But the man did not feed Faro. He did not make a fire, or eat any supper. But it may be that in the morning he will be better.

FIVE

May 27

I am writing in the morning, having eaten my breakfast; I am sitting at the entrance to the cave with my binoculars, watching the house and the tent for a sign of life. So far there has been none, except that the dog went to the tent again, wagged his tail again, and sat down expectantly for a minute or two. When nothing happened, he ran around the house, up the hill, and came to see me. Poor Faro. He was hungry, and now that he is home he expects to be fed. There is plenty of dog food in the store, but of course I have none up here, so I gave him a piece of corn bread and some canned hash. I could be gladder to see him this time, since for the moment at least I was not worried about the man. I patted him quite a bit, and talked to him. After he had eaten, he lay down beside me at the entrance and rested his head on my foot. That seemed quite touching because it is what he used to do with David, never with anyone else. Still, after only a few minutes, he got up and ran back down the hill. He emerged at the house, where he sat down near the entrance to the tent. Although he likes me, he seems to be adopting the man.

But the man himself has not moved.

I know he is sick, but I do not know how sick, and therefore I do not know what to do. It may be that he just doesn't feel very well and has decided to stay in bed.

Or he may be so sick he can't get up. He may even be dying.

Last night I would not have thought it would worry me so much, but this morning it does. It began with a dream I had just before I got up. It was one of those dreams that are more like daydreams; I have them when I am half-awake and half-asleep. I am somewhat aware that I am dreaming, and in a sense am making the dream up; but being half-asleep, it still seems true. I dreamed (or daydreamed) that it was my father in the tent, sick, and then that my whole family were there again, in the house. I felt so joyful it took my breath away, and I woke up.

I lay there realizing that it was not true, but also realizing something else. I thought I had become used to being alone, and to the idea that I would always be alone, but I was wrong. Now that somebody is here, the thought of going back, the thought of the house and the valley being empty again—this time forever, I am sure of that—seems so terrible I cannot bear it.

So, even though the man is a stranger and I am afraid of him, I am worrying about his being sick, and the idea that he might die makes me feel quite desperate.

I am writing this partly to get it clear in my head and to help me make up my mind. I think what I will do is wait and watch until late afternoon. Then if he still has not come out of the tent, I will go down while it is still light, very quietly, and see if I can see, without getting too close, how he is. I will take my gun with me.

May 28

I am back in the house, in my own room.

The man is in the tent. He is asleep, most of the time at least, and so sick he cannot get up. He scarcely knows I am here.

Yesterday afternoon at four o'clock, as I had decided, I took my gun and went down the hill to the house. I came up behind it and walked, slowly and quietly, listening, around to the front. If I heard any activity, I was going to duck back and try to get away again without being seen. When I reached the front yard, the dog came rushing up to meet me. I was afraid he was going to bark, but he did not, he just sniffed at my knee, wagged his tail, and watched. I crept to the tent and looked in. It has a flap to close it, but that was hanging loose, partly open. Still, it was dark inside. I could see only his legs at first. I crept closer, put my head inside, and my eyes adjusted to the dark. He lay on a sleeping bag, partly covered, his eyes closed, his head in a mess where he had been sick. He was breathing quite fast and shallow. Beside him lay a water bottle, a green plastic thing, knocked over and spilled; beside that lay a jar of pills, large white ones, with the top off, also knocked over and partly spilled out.

The tent roof was only about four feet high. I kneeled down and went in, just a little way, so I could reach his hand where it lay on top of the bag. The smell was terrible. I touched his hand: it was dry and hot with fever. Just as I touched it, Faro, his nose in the entrance, whined, and at the combination of the noise and the touch, he opened his eyes.

"Edward," he said. "Edward?"

He was not looking at me, or if he was, he was not seeing me; but I think he was looking at my gun, which I was still holding, because the next thing he said was:

"Bullets. It won't stop . . ." He did not finish the sentence, but sighed and closed his eyes again. He was dreaming; he was delirious, and his voice sounded thick, as if his throat and mouth were swollen.

"You're sick," I said. "You have a fever."

He moaned, and spoke without opening his eyes again. "Water. Please give me water."

I could see what had happened: before he collapsed, he had opened a bottle of water and some pills. In his confusion he had knocked them over. The bottle was empty, and he was too weak to get more.

"All right," I said, "I'll get you some water. It will take a few minutes."

I got a pail from the kitchen and ran to the stream where it flowed into the pond; the water is clearest there. When I got back, I was hot and out of breath; I had filled the pail nearly full and it was heavy. I got a cup from the house and dipped it half full.

He was asleep again, so I touched his shoulder.

"Here," I said, "drink this."

He tried to rise but could not, not even on his elbow; and when he tried to take the cup, he dropped it. I half filled it again from the pail; this time I held it and lifted his head a little with my other hand. He gulped it down; he was really thirsty.

"More," he said.

"Not now," I said. "It will make you sick again." I do not know much about medicine, but I know that much. He fell back and went to sleep again instantly.

The truth is, I do not know enough to take care of him. I helped my mother sometimes taking care of David or Joseph when they got sick (grippe, chicken pox,

47

things like that), but never anyone this sick. Still, there is no one else, so I have to try.

I got a rag from the house and, using some of the water, I cleaned up as well as I could around his head; I got him a fresh pillow and a clean blanket. I put the pills—those that were still clean—back in the bottle, capped it, and looked at the label: *Cysteamine*, whatever that is. The only medicine I have in the house (and the store) is aspirin and some cold tablets. But I wouldn't know what medicine to give him anyway if I had more.

I thought that since drinking the water had not made him sick again, perhaps he should eat something. But what? I decided on soup—chicken soup; that is what my mother usually gave us when we were sick. I had left some canned food in the house (it would have looked odd not to) when I moved to the cave, but there was no soup, so I had to walk to the store. I got some other stuff while I was there; I had already decided to move back to the house, but to leave the cave stocked for the time being, just in case. So I had quite a load to carry, and by the time I got back and got a fire going it was nearly dark.

When I took the soup in to him I found, to my surprise, that he seemed somewhat improved. He was awake, and when I entered he stared, quite bewildered, and with some effort managed to raise himself on one elbow. Then he spoke to me consciously for the first time. His voice was still very weak.

"I don't know where I am," he said. "Who are you?"

"You're in the valley," I said. "You've been sick."

I put the soup down beside him. I had thought I would have to feed it to him.

"The valley," he said. "I remember now. All the green trees. But there was no one there." He lay back on the pillow again.

"I was here," I said. "I stayed in the woods." (I thought it better not to mention the cave.) "Then I saw you were sick, and I thought you needed help."

"Sick," he said. "Yes, very sick."

"I made you some soup," I said. "Try to eat it."

He did try, but his hand was so weak he spilled it, so in the end I did feed it to him. He ate seven spoonfuls and then said, "No more. Too sick." He fell asleep again. However, I think even that bit of soup did him some good; he seemed to sleep more naturally and was not breathing so fast. I had brought a thermometer from the house to take his temperature, but I decided that could wait until morning. I touched his forehead. It was hot all right. From close up, in the dimness of the tent, he looked extremely frail.

I went back up to the cave, got my alarm clock and calendar, a lamp, this notebook, and some other things, and came back to the house. I set the alarm for midnight; when it went off, I reset it for two o'clock, then for four o'clock. Each time it rang I went out with a flashlight and looked in the tent to see how he was. Once he woke and asked again for water; I gave him a cupful. The rest of the time he slept steadily.

This morning I crumbled some of the remaining corn bread in some milk and took it to him for breakfast. (I had to use powdered milk because the cows are still out. I will have to catch them now and bring them back in. Also the chickens.)

This time he seemed very much better. His eyes have lost the dazed look they had earlier. He thanked me for the bread and milk and was able to spoon it out himself. After he finished eating it, he actually sat up for a moment; then he lay back again and said:

"I need to find out what made me sick."

"I think it is because you swam in Burden Creek," I said.

"Burden Creek?"

"The stream across the road."

"You know about that?"

"I was watching—from a distance away."

"You know about the water?"

"Nothing lives in it. I don't know just why."

"I discovered that. But not until the day after I took a bath in it. So stupid to be careless, after all this time. I had not been in water for a year. I was too eager. Still, I should have tested. But that other water, in the pond, was all right. So I thought . . ." He stopped and lay quietly for a time. Then he said:

"I might as well know. Could you—"

"Could I what?"

"Do you know what a Geiger counter is?"

"Those glass tubes you have."

"Yes. Can you read one?"

"No. That is, I never have."

I got the smaller of the tubes out of his wagon-trunk, and he showed me a gauge on one end of it, a small needle that wavered a bit when you moved it, like a compass. The dial was numbered from zero to 200. I took it across the road to Burden Creek. In the tent and crossing the road, the needle stayed at about 5. But when I got near the water it began to go up. Standing back as far as I could, I held it a foot above the stream. The needle *shot* over—up to about 180, almost as high as it could go. And he had been *in* the water. No wonder he got sick. I did not stay there, but got back across the road.

When I told him what the needle showed, he groaned and covered his eyes with his hand.

"One hundred eighty," he said. "And I was in the water at least ten minutes. My God. I must have got 300 rs. Maybe more."

"What does that mean?" I asked.

"It means I have radiation poisoning. Very bad."

"But you're getting better."

"It comes in stages."

He knew a great deal about radiation sickness; apparently he had studied it even before the war. The first

51

part, getting sick to your stomach, lasts only a day or so, then goes away. However, the radiation causes what he called intracellular ionization, and that is the real damage. It means that some of the molecules in his cells are destroyed, so that the cells no longer work normally and cannot grow and divide. In a short time—a day or two, maybe longer—he is going to get much sicker. He will get a very high fever, and since his blood cells were damaged and cannot reproduce, he will also get anemic. Worst of all, he will have no resistance to germs and infection; he will be very susceptible to pneumonia or even the mildest impurities in his food and water.

"How bad will it get?" I asked. What I meant, but did not want to say, was, are you likely to die? He understood.

"Do you know what an r means? It's a roentgen, a way of measuring radiation. If I absorbed 300 rs in that stream, I may live through it. If I got 400 or 500, well, then it's hopeless."

He said all this in a very matter-of-fact way; he was calm about it. I think I would have been hysterical. However, I tried to stay calm, too, and be practical.

So I said: "While you are feeling better, you should tell me all you can about what I should do. Do you have medicine to take? What should you eat?"

He looked at the jar of pills, still on the floor where I had put it. "Those won't help, not now. No, there's no medicine. In a hospital they give transfusions and intravenous nutrients."

I can't do that, of course. So what it amounts to is that there won't be much I can do, not until I see how the sickness develops. The only thing he seems sure of at this point is that he will have a very high fever and anemia. It is likely, but not certain, that he will develop some kind of infection like pneumonia or dysentery. One thing I can do will be to try to prevent that. I can boil and sterilize everything he eats and eats from—just as you do for a baby. When I get the cows and chickens back in, I can give him fresh milk and eggs to eat; they are nourishing and easy to digest.

And if he is strong enough to walk a little tomorrow, I will try to help him into the house. He can sleep in Joseph and David's room, on a bed. It will be dryer and warmer in the house, and easier for me to take care of him.

I just realized that, after all this, I still do not even know his name.

SIX

May 29

His name is John R. Loomis; he is a chemist from Ithaca, New York, where Cornell University is, or used to be.

He was much better this morning—so much so that I began to doubt whether he was really going to get sick again at all. But he said that is normal for radiation poisoning. And it turns out he is a real expert on the subject. In fact that is, in a way, how he happens to be alive at all, and how he was able to make his way here.

I woke up early, feeling very cheerful, thinking that there was someone to talk to even if he was sick. I got some more water, heated it over the fireplace and took a bath, something I haven't been able to do for a while. (I do it by carrying the warm water into the tub in the bathroom. You can wash quite well with just two bucketfuls once you get used to it.) Then I put on my good slacks. After all, he is "company" in a way, and I thought I should dress up a bit. I felt a little embarrassed at first when I looked in the mirror; but it was just because I am so used to the men's blue jeans.

Last night before I went to bed (in my own room again), I went out to the chicken yard, opened the gate, and scattered some chicken corn on the ground. This morning, after I was dressed, I went out and looked. Sure enough, they had come back in, and there were three fresh eggs in the hen house. I boiled them, toasted the last of the corn bread, made some coffee, and opened a can of tomato juice. It made a respectable-looking breakfast. I put it on a tray—also a jar of raspberry jam—and carried it out to the tent. The sun had just come over the ridge on the east, which meant it was about 8:30. Down the valley a couple of crows were calling. I felt happy and excited.

And to my surprise he was sitting up in the doorway of the tent.

"You're better," I said.

"For the moment," he said. "At least I think I can eat something."

I put the tray down in front of him, and he stared at it.

"Amazing," he said. He just whispered it.

55

"What?"

"This. Fresh eggs. Toast. Coffee. This valley. You, all by yourself. You are all by yourself?"

It was sort of a key question, and he looked a little suspicious as he asked it, as if I, or someone, might be playing a trick on him. Still, there wasn't any use pretending anything else.

"Yes."

"And you managed to stay alive, and raise chickens, eggs, and cows?"

"It hasn't been so hard."

"And the valley. How did it escape?"

"I don't really understand that. Except that people always used to say the valley had its own weather."

"A meteorological enclave. Some kind of an inversion. I suppose that's a theoretical possibility. But the odds—"

I said: "You'd better eat. It will all get cold."

If he was going to be too sick to eat later, he had better eat now and build up his strength. As for the valley, I had wondered enough about it, especially in the first few months when I was still expecting the deadness to creep in from outside. But it did not, and there was not much sense calling it a theoretical possibility when we were in it. At that point I did not know yet that he was a chemist, a scientist. And scientists won't just accept things—they always have to try to figure them out.

He ate his breakfast. Then, still sitting up, he told me his name. And, of course, I told him mine.

"Ann Burden," he said. "But weren't there other people living in the valley?"

"My family," I said. "And the people who owned the store, Mr. and Mrs. Klein."

And I told him about how they drove away and never came back. Also about the Amish, and what my father had seen in Ogdentown.

"I suppose they kept going too long," he said. "It's hard not to, especially at first. I know. You keep hoping. And of course, so soon after the war there was still the nerve gas."

"Nerve gas?"

"That's what killed most of the people. In a way it's better. They just went to sleep and never woke up."

It had taken him ten weeks to get from Ithaca to the valley, and all that way, all that time, he had seen no living thing—no people, no animals, no birds, no trees, not even insects—only gray wasteland, empty highways, and dead cities and towns. He had been ready to give up and turn back when he finally came over the ridge and saw, in the late evening, the haze of blue green. At first he thought it was a lake, and, like all the other lakes he had come upon, dead. But the next morning, by better light, he saw that this green was different, a color he had almost forgotten. As I had suspected, he still did not believe it, but came on to investigate anyway. Not until he came over Burden Hill did he know that he had finally found life. I had seen that for myself; that was when I first saw him.

He finished eating his breakfast; he ate it all and drank the coffee. But he was still weak and started back into the tent to lie down on his sleeping bag.

"Why do you sleep in the tent?" I said. "If you are going to be sick again, the house would be better."

He said: "The tent is radiation-proof."

"But there's no radiation in the valley," I said. "You've learned that."

"I have," he said. "But at first I didn't trust it."

"But you know now."

"I do," he said. "But now you've come back, and the house is yours."

"If you're sick, and I'm to take care of you, I can do it better in the house."

He did not argue any longer, but got up, very shaky on his legs, and walked a few steps toward the house. He stopped. "I'm quite dizzy," he said. "I'll have to rest."

"You can lean on me," I said.

He put his hand on my shoulder, leaning quite heavily, and after a few minutes we went on. It took about ten minutes of this to get him to the house, up the porch steps, and into Joseph and David's room, which fortunately is on the ground floor next to the living room. He lay on David's bed and went to sleep. I got him a blanket.

He slept until about noon, and during that time I went down to the far field, past the pond, to get the two cows and the calf and put them back into the pasture. They had grown used to their new freedom, however, and did not want to come with me, so in the end I had to cut a stick and drive them. Of course the calf kept running off in every direction, but eventually I did get the two cows in with the gate shut. A few minutes later the calf was bawling to get in, too. I got the fresh cow (its mother) into the barn and milked her. She is still giving almost a gallon at each milking. Just the same, she is bound to go dry within a year, and then we will have a milkless, creamless, butterless period for a while, until the bull calf grows up. I'm not even sure how long that will take.

When I got back to the house, Mr. Loomis was just waking, but he stayed in bed. I fixed some lunch, and then he told me some more of his story.

It began when he was a graduate student at Cornell. He was an organic chemist, doing research on plastics and polymers. (He explained that these are very long molecules used in making nylon, Dacron, and the stretchy kind of plastic wrap.) The head of the department in which he studied was a Professor Kylmer, a very famous man who had once won a Nobel prize.

Professor Kylmer had a research grant from the government and worked part of the time at a special laboratory they had built for him, not at Cornell but in the mountains about twenty miles away. The whole thing was secret, but it had something to do with plastic and polymers, which were also the professor's specialty.

Mr. Loomis knew the professor fairly well (being his pupil), though he was always completely wrapped up in his work and not a very friendly man. One day, however, he invited Mr. Loomis into his private office in the Cornell chemistry building. He was obviously excited over something. He asked Mr. Loomis, as soon as the door was shut, if he would like to come and work with him in the secret laboratory. He said that he had just made an important discovery and needed to increase his staff. Mr. Loomis, after thinking it over, accepted the offer—since, as the professor explained, it was the same kind of research he was doing anyway, and this way he would get paid for doing it.

The discovery was a method of magnetizing plastic. Mr. Loomis called it "polarizing," but that means making it magnetic. Since the plastic was made of polymers, they called it "polapoly."

That did not sound like too exciting a discovery to me, but when he explained what it was for, I could see that it was—or would seem so to the government. The point was that magnetism can stop, or at least turn aside, radiation. Mr. Loomis reminded me (I had learned it in school) that it is the earth's magnetic field that keeps us all from being killed by cosmic rays. So a magnetic plastic could be used to make a radiation-proof suit.

That was what the government—the army, of course

—wanted. So that troops could live on (*fight on!*) in places that had been atom-bombed. The government would issue suits to civilians, too, eventually, but the army wanted the first ones.

This happened about three years before the war. The laboratory to which Mr. Loomis reported the next day was eighty feet underground, a place as big as a house, hollowed out of a mountainside of solid rock. He worked there almost every day for the next three years, and often slept there, too. There were living quarters so that when they got busy on some crucial test they did not need to drive back to Ithaca. They had stores of food and even a kitchen.

He soon learned that the project was more complicated than just making a plastic suit. There wasn't much point in giving a soldier a safe-suit if he could not breathe the air around him, or drink the water. (Food rations, even cases of food, they could wrap in the plastic.) But Professor Kylmer had already started working on a variation of the plastic—a thin, slightly porous membrane that you could filter water through. It worked this way: the worse the water was, the less you got, but what did come through was pure; the filter would not pass the radioactive part. Then they designed a similar membrane for air. That was harder, because the clean air had to be trapped and compressed into a tank. But they worked it out, all in a compact unit that a man could carry and operate with a hand pump.

These were (I now realized) the things Mr. Loomis

had brought with him—the greenish suit he was wearing when I first saw him, the air tank on his back; the water filter and a supply of purified water had been in the wagon-trunk. The tent, of course, was made of the same stuff as the suit, and so was the trunk itself.

They had designed all these in the laboratory and finished a single pilot model of each just before the war began. A report had been sent to Washington, and a team was coming from the Pentagon to test everything. If it was all okay they were to start production in plastics factories all over the country.

But the men from the Pentagon never got there. It was all too late. The war broke out and was over before a single safe-suit was ever issued to a single soldier, much less to a civilian.

On the night the bombing began, Mr. Loomis was working late in the laboratory. He heard the news on the radio, and he decided to stay there, at least for the time being, to see how things went. He had a good supply of food—mostly army rations of freeze-dried things (which would keep indefinitely), for they had been testing the plastic for food packaging. Professor Kylmer was not there; he had gone back to Ithaca, and Mr. Loomis never saw him again.

In the laboratory, Mr. Loomis also had the world's only radiation-proof suit, and he had the air filter and the water filter.

Like me, he heard the radio stations go off one by one.

Still he thought there might be other survivors in underground places like his—the Air Force, for instance, was supposed to have several shelters, all equipped so that the men in them could last for months. The difference was that if they *were* alive, they could not go out, and he could.

He stayed in the laboratory for three months, hoping the radiation level in the air outside would go down, but it did not. Then he began a series of expeditions. At first they were short ones. The suit had been carefully tested in the laboratory, and it was safe against all predictable radiation levels. But it had never actually been used "in the field"; so he was cautious, and it was lucky he was. His first impulse, for instance, was to get into his car and drive to Ithaca, the nearest big town. Before he did, he checked the radioactivity inside the car, using a Geiger counter from the laboratory. He discovered it was *ten times* as high as it was in the open air: apparently the metal body, reflecting the radioactivity inward from six directions, concentrated the rays more than anyone had anticipated. Anyway, the level was too near the theoretical limit of what the suit could handle for him to risk it.

Since then he had tested hundreds of cars, and they were all the same—as he said, too hot to be safe. Even motorcycles were dangerous. Bicycles were better, but too difficult to ride in the bulky plastic suit. So he ended up walking and hauling his supplies in the wagon-trunk, which he had made himself, out of bicycle parts and a big, light plywood carton covered with polapoly.

His first long trip was to the west, to Chicago, where he knew there had been an underground Air Force command post. Using a map, he had calculated the distance he had to cover each day, how long it would take, and how much freeze-dried food he would need. He knew he would not find anything edible along the way; there might be usable food at the underground post itself, but he could not count on that.

He found the Air Force base all right, barricaded, walled, fenced, with KEEP OUT signs starting a mile away. It was a shambles. Apparently men stationed in the barracks outside had tried to fight their way into the safe-room; local civilians had joined them, and in the battle grenades had been used. There were bodies everywhere outside and just inside, with no sign of life. He tried to take the elevator down to the safe-room, but it did not work. Taking a flashlight from his trunk, he climbed instead down a steep, ladderlike stairway. After the first ten steps it was totally dark.

The command room itself, ninety steps farther down, was relatively undamaged: a large oval room with maps on the walls, desks, telephones, and a bank of computers. Three dead men in uniforms sat slumped over their desks; each had a loaded rifle next to him. Yet they had not been shot. They had died, Mr. Loomis guessed, of asphyxiation; they would have depended for air on a bottled oxygen-mix, and someone, somewhere in the underground maze, had wrecked the circulation pumps.

In the end, he decided it really did not matter so much. Because all of the underground fallout shelters, this one and others around the world, had built-in time limits, enough air and water to last three months, six months, a year, on the assumption that after that it would be safe to go outside again. And that had not happened.

Mr. Loomis had been telling all this as he lay in David's bed, having finished eating his lunch. I could see that he was anxious to tell it, but that he was getting tired. When he finished what I have written here, he reached to get a drink of water from the glass I had put on his lunch tray, but the glass was empty. I took the tray away to the kitchen, and the glass with it. I refilled it, and while I was taking it back I remembered one more thing I was really curious about.

I gave him the water and asked: "Who was Edward?" Because that was the name he had called me when he first saw me in the tent, when he was delirious.

For a second after I asked the question I thought the sickness had come back on him, because his eyes got a wild look again, as if he were seeing a nightmare. The hand holding the glass of water opened, and the glass slipped and fell to the floor. At the noise it made, he shook his head and his eyes unclouded. Still he stared.

"How do you know about Edward?"

"When I first saw you," I said, "in the tent, you called me Edward. Is something wrong? Are you sick?"

He relaxed. "It was a shock," he said. "Edward was a man who worked in the laboratory with Dr. Kylmer and me. But I didn't think I had mentioned his name."

I got him another glass of water, and cleaned up the floor where the first one had fallen.

SEVEN

June 3

Four days have passed.

On the first day, Mr. Loomis's condition remained about the same. I gave him the fever thermometer, and we began keeping track of his temperature. It was about 99.5 degrees in the morning, went up to 101 in the middle of the day, and fell back to 99.5 in the evening. He said that meant he was still in the "interim" period.

I thought he should take some aspirin, but he said it would not do any real good, and that we should save it—the half-dozen bottles in the store being perhaps the only usable aspirin left in the world. He said it seriously, but I had a feeling he was half-joking.

I had a lot to do. With him in the valley—in the house—I decided I should cook better meals than I did when I was by myself. For one thing, as I said, if he was going to be sick, he ought to build up his strength. Anyway, I like to cook, but when I was alone I frequently just did not bother—it seemed silly just for one.

So I made several trips to the store for supplies. It was all canned stuff, of course, or dried. There would not be anything fresh except milk and eggs until I could get the garden going again. Since it was already June, that was the most urgent thing. I wished now I had not dug it all up—I could be having fresh greens right now. Also the lettuce would have been ready. It was probably too late to start either of those again, but I decided to try anyway, in the hope that it would stay cool. I could at least get some to seed for next year. But I really longed for a salad and fresh greens.

I got the spade and the hoe and went to work. Faro came up and sniffed the first few shovelfuls of earth I turned over. Then he dug a small hole of his own and lay on top of it. It was warm in the sun. He is already looking much better than he did at first.

It was easy spading, since the dirt had already been turned up once; also the manure was still in it, so I did not have to haul that again. I had plenty of seeds; I had taken them up to the cave with me when I moved. But after I had turned up the whole patch—in fact after I had it partly planted—I realized that it was really not big enough. Because, of course, with two we would need twice as much of everything, and I wanted some left over for preserving. The canned stuff in the store is not going to last forever. So I decided to double the size of the garden.

There was plenty of room, but for the new part I had to spade through turf, which was much harder digging. Still, I was making pretty good progress when I noticed Faro standing up and wagging his tail. I looked up and there, leaning against the gatepost watching me, was Mr. Loomis. I had left him after lunch, still lying on David's bed. It was now late afternoon, almost time to stop and get the dinner. I was somewhat ashamed to have him see me, because working so hard I was dirty, hot, and sweaty. I had intended to clean up before I went into his room.

But more, I was concerned. What was he doing out here, out of bed? I walked over, still carrying the spade, and asked, "Is something wrong?"

"Nothing wrong," he said. "I was feeling bored. It's a warm afternoon, so I came out."

I had forgotten about being bored. There was always so much to do. But of course I had not been sick in bed. I had given him some books to read, but they were historical novels that used to be my mother's. I suppose he did not like them much. I had some more books in my bedroom upstairs, but they were mostly either school books or children's books. We generally depended on the public library in Ogdentown.

"I've been digging," I said, which of course he had already seen. "This is going to be the garden."

"Hard work for a girl," he said, noticing, I suppose, how messy I looked.

"I'm used to it." I started to tell him that most of it had already been dug before and was therefore easy, but then I decided not to. I did not want him to know how afraid I had been when I first saw him coming.

He looked puzzled. "But do you have to do it all by hand? Didn't your father have a tractor?"

"It's in the barn."

"You can't run it?"

"I can, but there's no gasoline."

"But there are two gasoline pumps at the store. There must be gas there."

That was true. The Amish, though they did not drive cars, used plenty of tractors, reapers, balers, and other machines, and bought their gas from Mr. Klein.

"I suppose there is," I said. "But the pumps won't work without electricity."

"And you've been doing all this with a shovel. Don't you realize it would be simple to take the motors off the pumps and work them by hand? There may be four or five thousand gallons there." He smiled, but it made me feel stupid.

"I don't know much about electric motors and pumps," I said.

"But I do," he said. "At least enough to do that."

"When you're well again," I said.

Without having discussed it, we both had begun going on the assumption that he would recover.

I was really glad to hear what he said about the gasoline and the tractor, and I hoped it would work. There was enough winter pasture for the three cows, but just barely. With the tractor running I could mow the grass after it went to seed, and bring in some hay. Also, I hoped eventually to increase the herd.

We walked back to the house just as the sun was setting. Because the walls of the valley are so high, the sun always sets early and rises late; there is a long twilight, and we never have really big sunsets the way they do where the land is level. Still this was one of the better ones. My father used to say, "In a valley the real sunset is in the east," and that is how it was. As the sun disappeared over the west ridge, the last of the orange light moved up the hill on the east, with the darker shadow climbing up after it. At the end only the tops of the last high trees were lit, and they looked as if they were burning. Then they faded and went out, and it was dusk.

We stopped a minute to watch it, and he rested his hand on my shoulder as he had on the gatepost. I felt proud to be of help to him, but when we turned to walk the rest of the way, he went alone. He was obviously much stronger and standing straighter. I realized that he was quite tall.

It turned colder that night, so after we had eaten dinner I built a fire in the living room fireplace and closed the windows. Since the living room adjoins his—Joseph and David's—room, I opened the door so the fire would warm it, too. He did not go back into the bedroom immediately, however, but sat down in a chair near the fireplace.

The living room has two big upholstered chairs and a sofa, all placed so you can see the fire, which my father and mother liked to do in winter. (This last winter I slept on the sofa to be near the fire.) The chair Mr. Loomis sat in was the one my father used to use. The electric lamps are still beside the chairs—I left them there for looks, even though they will not light. Against the wall on one side of the room stands the phonograph, and against the other our piano.

"Would you like me to get you a book?" I said, thinking he would be bored again. "I can put the lamp on the table by the chair."

He said: "No, thank you. I only want to look at the fire a few minutes. Then I'll get sleepy. The fire always does that."

Still, for the first time it bothered me. There was absolutely nothing for him to do. When I am by myself—when I *was* by myself—I was always quite tired at the end of the day, and unless I had washing or sewing or something like that to do, I usually went to sleep very soon after eating. Now I wished there was a radio station to tune in, or that the phonograph would work. It was quite a good one, and we had a lot of records. But it would not play without electricity so I did something I would be embarrassed to do under ordinary circumstances. I said, "Would you like me to play the piano?" I added quickly, "I can't play very well."

To my surprise he seemed extremely pleased, almost excited. "*Could* you?" he said. "I haven't heard music for more than a year."

I felt sorry for him, because I not only can't play too well, but I don't have much music. I have the John Thompson *Second Year Lesson Book*, Thompson's *Easy Pieces*, and a recital piece I once learned, *Für Elise*. The lesson book is about half-finger exercises.

I put the lamp near the piano and started on *Easy Pieces*. A lot of them are too babyish, but toward the end of the book there are some harder ones that are quite pretty. I played these, glancing at him now and then. He really seemed to like it, and I guess because of that I played better than I usually do, and hardly made any mistakes. I mean, he didn't clap or say anything, but he sat forward in his chair and listened without moving at all. When I finished *Easy Pieces*, I played *Für Elise*, then a few things from the lesson book, and that was all I had, except hymns.

I can play hymns better than anything else, because I used to play them for our Sunday School singing. I opened the hymn book and played two of my favorites, "How Great Thou Art" and "In the Garden." The melodies are good, but the arrangements are not really meant for the piano, but for singing. I played "In the Garden" very softly, and when I looked around again he had fallen asleep, still leaning forward in his chair. I was afraid he would fall, so I stopped, and when I did he woke up.

"Thank you," he said. "That was beautiful." He waited, and then added, "This is the best evening I ever spent."

I said: "Ever? You mean since the war."

"You heard me," he said. "I said 'ever.' " He sounded angry. Of course, he has a fever and doesn't feel well.

He went to bed then; I told him to leave the bedroom door open, and I put some more wood on the fire, thick logs that would last all night. Then I went upstairs to my bedroom. It had turned surprisingly cold, not like winter, but sharp just the same. I had a couple of blankets, and I lay there on the bed thinking and trying to warm up.

For some reason, playing the hymns had made me feel sad, as if I were homesick even though I was at home. They made me think of Sunday School. When we went to school, regular school, we went on the bus with other children; but when we went to Sunday School we drove to Ogdentown in the car with my mother and father, dressed in our good clothes, and it was always festive. I remember so many things about it. I started when I was two; it was my nursery school and kindergarten; I learned the alphabet there, from a picture book called *The Bible Letter Book.*

The first page said "A is for Adam," and there was a picture of Adam standing near an apple tree, dressed in a long white robe—which disagrees with the Bible, but of course it was for small children. Next came "B is for Benjamin." "C is for Christian," and so on. The last page of all was "Z is for Zachariah," and since I knew that Adam was the first man, for a long time I assumed that Zachariah must be the last man. I learned all the letters from that book, so that by the time I went to regular school I could already read a little.

Thinking about Sunday School and about Mr. Loomis getting angry, I wished I were back in the cave again. It seemed cozier somehow. Finally, I decided to go sleep there (I had left some blankets and stuff up there) and come back early enough so that Mr. Loomis would not know I had been away. I got up and started walking down the stairs toward the hallway and the door. As I passed the bedroom door where he was sleeping, I heard a shout, and then another. He was talking loudly, but I could not hear what he was saying. His voice sounded troubled and I thought he might need help.

So I went back closer to the door. He was dreaming, a bad dream I could tell, a nightmare. He was talking in outbursts, sometimes quite angrily. Then he would stop, as if listening for an answer. I realized I was hearing half of a conversation. It was not all clear, but he was talking to Edward.

He said: "In charge. In charge of what?"

There was a pause.

Then he said: "Not anymore, Edward. It doesn't mean anything now."

Another pause.

"What good can it do? We know they're dead. There isn't a chance. Can't you grasp that? Mary is *dead*. Billy is dead. You can't help them."

This went on, his voice gradually growing quieter, finally dropping to a mumble that I could not hear.

Then he shouted again, a very urgent shout: "Get away. I warn you. Get away from ——" The last word I could not understand. And after that he gave a terrible groan, so painful I thought he must be hurt.

And then silence.

I crept to the door of the bedroom and listened. He was breathing regularly and quietly. Whatever the nightmare had been, it was over. Still, I was worried. Was it just a nightmare, or was he delirious again? I was afraid the sickness might be coming back.

I decided I had better not go to the cave after all. Suppose he should call for help?

I went back upstairs and rolled up in the blankets. A little later there was a whining outside my door. I opened it and let Faro in. He lay down next to me on the bed, and after a while I went to sleep.

EIGHT

June 3, continued

I woke up before dawn with an inspiration: an idea
how to make a salad. What brought it to me was a dream
I was having of my mother carrying a wicker basket,
walking across a field and into a woods. When I woke, I
realized what she was doing. She was getting cress,
dandelion greens, and poke greens, as she always did
early in June. On the edge of the far field, beyond the
pond, they grow wild; field cress looks about like water-
cress and, mixed with dandelion greens, it makes good
green salad. The poke greens you have to cook, but
when they are young they are rather like spinach (when

they get old, however, they are bitter and can be poisonous). My mother used to gather them every spring, carrying a basket to put them in, and David, Joseph, and I used to go with her—and Faro, of course. I had forgotten all about that until now, which shows that dreams can be helpful.

I got excited about the idea and jumped out of bed. I knew exactly where the basket was, on a shelf in the kitchen cupboard, and where the greens grew. Not only was I hungry for greens, but I thought Mr. Loomis must be even hungrier, since he could not possibly have eaten anything like that in more than a year, while I at least had had last summer's garden. I started to get the basket, and then I remembered his nightmare, and my worry that he might be sick, so I went downstairs very quietly and listened outside his bedroom door, which was still open. He seemed to be sleeping peacefully. His breathing was quiet and even. So I decided it was safe to go. I would not be gone very long anyway. I took the basket from the shelf, got a glass of milk from the cellar (where I keep it, with the eggs and butter, because it is always cold), drank it, and went out. I would cook breakfast later.

It was cool, but still and pleasant, not yet very light though it was almost seven o'clock. The sun would not come over the ridge until about eight. I walked along the road past the pond and then turned left across the field. Faro came with me, sniffing everything. The grass was wet and my sneakers quickly got soaked through; so did the bottoms of my blue jeans, so I rolled them up to my knees. Still I felt happy. Behind me in the pond I heard a big fish, a bass, jump and fall back into the water with a thump. I thought: after I get the cress and the other greens I will cook breakfast and then go fishing. With luck I might catch a bass or two to have for dinner with the salad. I would make a dressing of oil and vinegar, and cook some fresh biscuits.

I was getting near the far side of the field when all of a sudden Faro came to a point—tail straight, paw lifted, nose forward. I was amazed. Could it be possible that there were quail still in the valley? I could not believe it; I had heard none, and they have a call that cannot be mistaken. I inched forward behind the dog, and a rabbit went bounding away in the high grass. David used to scold Faro for pointing rabbits, but I did not. After all, there was nothing else to point, and rabbits are good to eat. So I patted him instead, and said, "Good Faro." I knew he was disappointed that I had no gun.

I found the field cress and dandelions, and beyond, where the woods began, the poke, just out of the ground, young and edible. In half an hour I had picked enough to fill the basket; I could have filled two. Then I had an illusion. The basket of green leaves suddenly seemed to be giving off a beautiful, sweet perfume. But that was impossible, so I looked around to see where the smell was coming from, and there, twenty feet ahead of me on the edge of the woods, was a crab-apple tree in full bloom.

I had known the tree was there; we used to eat the apples sometimes, and my mother used them for jelly. They had a nice flavor, though they were small, hard and quite sour. (There are better eating apple trees behind the barn.)

But I had never known the tree to look so beautiful or smell so nice. I supposed it seemed that way because the air was still and the fragrance just hung there, concentrated instead of blowing away on the wind. And because the light was still dim, a morning twilight, the branches and all the white blossoms looked misty and delicate, an almost magic look. I walked a few steps closer and then sat down, right in the wet grass, to stare. I thought, if I ever got married, apple blossoms were what I would like to have in the church. Which meant that I would have to get married in May or early June.

I got to thinking about it. Next June I would be seventeen, and in my entire life I had only had one real date, and that was when I was thirteen, in junior-high school. A boy named Howard Peterson asked me to go with him to a dance at the school. My mother took me— it was in Ogdentown—and stayed for the whole dance, sitting on the side with some other mothers. The only way you could tell it was a "date" was that Howard paid for both the tickets, fifty cents each. I have had other boyfriends, but I only saw them at school, or after school. The truth is, in high school most of the boys lived in Ogdentown, and those of us who came on the bus were regarded as outsiders—hillbillies, in fact, and not fashionable.

So to me the idea of getting married seemed like quite an enormous step. Still I thought, when Mr. Loomis recovered from his sickness, there was no reason why we could not plan to be married in a year; that is, next June, perhaps on my seventeenth birthday. I knew there could not be any minister, but the marriage ceremony was all written out in the back of the hymnal. There *should* be a ceremony; I felt strongly about that, and it should be in the church, on a definite date, with flowers. The whole idea was thrilling. I thought I might even wear my mother's wedding dress. I know where it is, folded up in a box in her closet.

Then it occurred to me: Mr. Loomis had not indicated the slightest interest in any such idea. But of course it was much too soon, and he was very sick. We would talk about it when he had finally recovered.

And I thought: what would it be like, ten years from now, to be up here gathering greens some morning with children of my own? But that thought made me feel lonesome for my mother, a feeling I have tried hard to avoid. So I stood up to change the subject. I got out my pocketknife and cut a bunch of apple blossoms. Mr. Loomis could have a bouquet for his sickroom.

I started back to the house. On the way, the sun

appeared over the ridge, but some clouds followed it almost immediately, and the chill stayed in the air. That was good, because I still had the rest of the garden to plant, and since it was late in the season, the cooler the weather stayed the better it would do.

At the house everything was quiet. I put the flowers in a vase and the greens in the cold cellar; they would be for dinner, in the nature of a surprise. Then I cooked breakfast—eggs, canned ham, and some pan biscuits. I really wished then that I had that wood stove moved in from the barn so that I could have a real oven and do some proper baking. I decided that I'd try those bolts soon and see if I could dismantle it.

I put the breakfast and the vase of flowers on a tray and knocked on his door, which was partly open. There was no answer so I pushed it wider, looked in, and learned why the house was so quiet—he was not there.

Immediately I was worried, very worried. I realized that it was stupid of me to have left him alone, knowing that he had had the nightmare, knowing that it might have been the beginning of the high fever. He might be, right now, wandering somewhere in a delirium. In the house? I called, but there was no answer. I put the tray down, setting the breakfast near the fire where it would stay warm, and ran to the front door.

It was all right. I saw him immediately, across the road not far from Burden Creek, sitting on a large round stone. He had the Geiger counter with him, the one with the earphone; he was staring at the creek, looking up-stream.

I walked over to him, and he looked up when he saw me coming. He said: "I thought you had run away."

"Are you all right?" I was still worried.

"Yes," he said. "In fact I woke up feeling so much better that I began to wonder about this water—whether maybe you had read the meter wrong, or whether the counter was off. So I walked over to check it with this one."

Oh, I hoped I had read it wrong! I had never hoped anything so much.

But I had not. He went on: "It was no use. Your reading was right. There's just no way I could have got less than 300 rs." He must have felt disappointed, but he said it calmly, as before; he did not sound frightened.

I said: "I wish I had been wrong."

"It's no worse than before," he said. "It was just a hope. Anyway, since you weren't here, I sat down and started thinking about that stream."

"Thinking what?"

"It's radioactive, there's no doubt about that. But that's no reason it shouldn't be useful. Up there"—he pointed to a place a hundred feet upstream, a rocky place where a big boulder blocked the creek and made a little waterfall—"there's a sort of a natural dam. It looks as if somebody, sometime, even tried to add to it."

"That's true," I said. "My father said that my great-

83

grandfather had a small mill there, a flour mill. He thought the stone you're sitting on was part of it, it's worn so smooth."

"What I was thinking about was not a mill, but electricity. If I could build that dam up a few feet higher— there's a good flow of water. It could run a small generator."

"But we don't have any generator. Anyway, if we tried to build a dam, we'd get the water on ourselves. It's too dangerous."

"Not if I was wearing the safe-suit, and if I was careful. And the generator is easy. You can make one out of any electric motor—with a little tinkering."

"But where would we get an electric motor?" Then I remembered. There were two or three of them in the barn, in my father's workshop. One, I know, was hooked up to a grindstone, another to a circular saw. I told Mr. Loomis, and he smiled.

"There are always motors around a farm. The hard part will be the waterwheel. But I think I can make one. I'll need some lumber and some kind of an axle. It won't be fancy, but it will work."

"Would it light the lights?"

"Yes. They might be a bit flickery, but they'd light. Mainly, it would run your refrigerator, your freezer, things like that. They don't use much current."

It would be nice to have a refrigerator again. And a freezer! I could freeze vegetables and fruit for the winter.

That reminded me. His breakfast was drying up by the fire. And I had had nothing to eat yet myself, except some milk and a couple of sprigs of field cress.

After breakfast I milked the cow and planted some more of the garden: melons, beets, and several rows of beans. I had some seed potatoes left; they looked pretty dried up, but I felt so optimistic and energetic I planted them anyway. They might revive.

Then I went to the house to get my fishing rod and to tell Mr. Loomis (lying down) I was going to the pond.

He sat up on the side of the bed.

He said: "Do you think—" I waited. "Well, I'd like to go with you."

"To fish?" I was torn. It would be fun to have him go, but the pond is more than a quarter of a mile off. "How is your fever?"

"About the same. About a hundred, not so bad."

"It's chilly out."

"I could take a blanket."

"I'll get you a coat." In the hall closet I found an old cloth raincoat of my father's. I thought it would not do him any harm, and it was something for him to do.

"Do you really want to fish?" I asked him.

He looked embarrassed. "I never have. I don't know how."

"I can show you. It's very easy, at least the way I do it. I just put a worm on the hook and throw it in. Sometimes I use a float, sometimes not."

"A float?" He *really* did not know how to fish.

"A little ball made of cork." I pulled one out of my pocket and showed him. "It keeps the hook off the bottom."

"Have you got an extra one?"

"Yes," I said, "and I can get David's rod." It was in his closet.

We started out for the pond, with him wearing my father's coat and carrying David's fishing pole. But we did not make it. After about a hundred yards he began walking very slowly; soon he stumbled and dropped the rod.

"I'm sorry," he said. "I can't go on." He had turned extremely pale, a bluish color. He looked terrible.

"Lean on me," I said. "Leave the rod. We'll go back."

"It's the anemia," he said. "I should have known. It's the dependable part of the disease. Five to seven days after exposure. This is the seventh day."

We started back, very slowly. He could hardly stand up.

I said: "You'd better lie down."

"Yes." He sank to the grass at the side of the road, lay on his back, and closed his eyes. But his color slowly got better.

"It came so suddenly," I said.

"No. It was the walking. I knew I had it a little."

"What should I do?"

"Nothing. Help me back to the house. Then go fishing."

So I did that. When we got back to the house, I sat beside his bed for a while, and then went on to the pond. But it was a nervous and disappointed kind of fishing. He had explained that the anemia would not get any worse, but it meant that he would not be able to do much now until he had gone through the whole illness and recovered. Then it should gradually go away. Still, I felt as if it was the beginning of the end—no, not the end, but of a bad time, and all my plans of this morning seemed thoughtless and foolish.

I fished just long enough to catch three bass, about half an hour. Fortunately they were biting. Then I went back.

He did seem better again, and even got up and sat at the table for lunch, though I noticed that he moved slowly and rather cautiously, and after he had eaten he lay down again immediately. When I looked into the bedroom a little later, he was asleep. I put a fresh glass of water by his bed.

I kept thinking about the stove. So while he slept I went down to the barn, got from my father's workshop a wrench, a pliers, a screwdriver, and a hammer, and went to work. To my surprise the stove came apart fairly easily—the oil I had put on the bolts last winter had done the trick. Even so I broke a couple of fingernails; but by sunset I had it lying in pieces on the barn floor. I found I could lift all of the pieces but one—the big cast-iron firebox. Even with the grates and door removed that was too heavy. However, I could turn it end over end, and by doing that get it onto a sheet of masonite I found in my father's workshop. Since the masonite is slick on one side (I made sure that side was down), I could drag it a ways, using the masonite as a sled. I intended to back the cart right up to the barn door, and try to get the grate that far on the sled, and then onto the cart. If I couldn't, I would just have to wait until Mr. Loomis was well and could help. I did not actually try it, because by the time I had it ready it was time to milk the cow, then clean up and start the dinner.

In spite of everything, dinner was festive, with the bass, the fresh-cooked greens, and the salad. It is incredible how good fresh green things can taste when you have not had any for months—or, in Mr. Loomis's case, more than a year. I set the table with the "good" china that my mother saved for Sundays, Christmas, Thanksgiving, and birthdays. I did forget one thing—candles. I had had some in the house but took them to the cave. There are more at the store, but I did not think of it until too late. However, the oil lamps gave a pleasant light. They just did not look as romantic. We ate all of the bass and all of the greens and salad, though there was enough for four.

After dinner, it being still cool, I built up the fire again. I had found some books that interested Mr. Loomis, a set called *The Farm Mechanic*. I had discovered them on a shelf in the workshop in the barn.

The set was an annual publication, like the *World Almanac*, and each is full of diagrams of motors, wiring systems, pumps, silos, balers, and so on. He studied them (there were eight volumes) for a long time. I could tell he was figuring out how to build the generator, and maybe making other plans as well.

NINE

June 3, continued

The next morning, amazingly enough, I got the tractor running. That was a direct result of *The Farm Mechanic*.

When I had finished cooking breakfast, I found Mr. Loomis on his bed, up on his elbow, reading one of the volumes, and he showed it to me. It was a set of diagram drawings of the inside mechanism of a gasoline pump—approximately identical to the ones at Mr. Klein's store. When I thought about it, finding the picture was not surprising; a great many farms, especially big ones, have their own gas pumps. I remembered that three or four of the Amish farms did, for example. So it was natural that farmers would need to know how to repair them.

"Look at this," Mr. Loomis said, pointing to one of the drawings. It showed the wheel of a small electric motor connected by a belt to a larger wheel. "That wheel runs the actual pump," he said, "and look at this." In the diagram, an arrow pointed to a small circular hole near the rim of the larger wheel. At the nonpointed end of the arrow was the number "7" with a circle around it.

"Now look at number seven in the table." Below the drawing there were printed instructions. Instruction number seven said: "Attach handle 'H' here for manual operation in case of power failure or in areas where electricity is unavailable. Remove V belt."

"What's 'handle H'?" I said.

He showed me another drawing across the page. "Handle H" turned out to be a knob, rather like a doorknob, with a pin on the end that would fit into "Hole 7" in the wheel. It seemed simple enough. That would convert the wheel into a sort of crank.

I said: "And if I turn it, gasoline will come out?"

"Say a prayer first. Gasoline *should* come out. Be sure to take off the belt."

"How?"

"Pry it off with a screwdriver."

"I could just cut it."

"No." He sounded most emphatic. "V belts are useful, and we have no place to buy any more."

I went to the store and examined (for the first time!) the gas pumps that stood in front of it, ordinary red-and-white things I had walked past a thousand times, one High-test, one Regular. The front, I now saw, was made like a door, with hinges on one side, but screwed shut. I got a screwdriver from the store and took out the screw; after prying a bit, the door came open rather squeakily. Inside all was as the diagram showed—the motor, the belt, the wheel, some pipes leading down. And there, clipped to the door in a spring-clamp, was "Handle H."

I tried to pry the belt loose from the wheels, but it was made of heavy, stiff rubber, very tight. Finally I had to take out some screws and remove the wheel from the motor, took off the belt, then replaced the wheel and the belt on it, so it would be there when we needed it.

Quite excited, I took "Handle H" from its clamp and inserted it into the slot on the big wheel (about fourteen inches in diameter). I unhooked the hose from the gas pump, and holding the nozzle in one hand and the knob in the other, I was ready to turn it. Which way? An arrow on the wheel pointed counterclockwise. I turned, and in ten seconds liquid was splashing in the gravel at my feet. The smell could not be mistaken—it was gasoline.

I stopped pumping and got a five-gallon container from the store and filled it. With the can bumping my leg every step, I carried it to the barn and filled the tractor's gas tank. I checked the oil—it was all right.

There was a self starter, but the battery was dead, of course. That had happened many times before, however, and I knew how to start it with the crank. First I primed the carburetor as my father had showed me (we all used to drive the tractor, starting at about age eight); then, saying the prayer I had forgotten to say at the gas pump, I cranked hard. The motor started immediately, with a loud, sputtering roar, and I felt like patting it on the hood. In fact, I did. The noise seemed incredibly loud. You forget how noisy machines are after a year.

The noise was partly because the tractor was still in the barn. I climbed up to the seat, put it in reverse, and backed it out. It was a bit less deafening. Though I was sure Mr. Loomis had heard it, I wanted him to see it, too, so I drove the tractor to the house and parked it outside his window. I almost laughed, remembering how I had hated to drive it several years ago; the girls who lived in Ogdentown didn't drive tractors. Now I could rejoice over the time and labor it would save us, and I hurried into the house to share the triumph.

He was sitting on the edge of the bed and was surprisingly matter-of-fact.

"You found Handle H," he said.

"And the gas came out on the first turn," I said. "I think that tank must be full."

"If it is, we have three thousand gallons. At least that's what *The Farm Mechanic* says—for a standard underground tank."

And in my excitement I had not even tried the other

pump. There might be six thousand!

I took the tractor back down to the barn and hitched on the plow. I had already decided what I was going to do. As you head back from the house to the barn, the pasture, the far field, the pond and the brook all lie on your right. To the left there are a few fruit trees and then, farther left, another small field of about an acre and a half. This was a field my father used for a few years to grow melons, pumpkins, squash, things like that, to sell in Ogdentown. However, he gave that up, as he said, because it did not make enough money to be worth the time it took. That was about five years ago; after that he merely kept the field mowed but not planted.

I had decided, if I got the tractor running, to plow that field and plant it in corn, with maybe a few rows of soybeans and pea beans. These were all staples that would take up too much room in the small vegetable garden near the house. Corn could be eaten by us, by the chickens, and, if there was any left over, by the cows—stalks and all.

The truth was, now that the tractor was running I could face a fact that I had previously tried to keep out of my mind, it being too depressing to dwell on: the store was an illusion.

It seemed, especially at first, like an endless supply of almost everything I needed. But in fact I knew it was not. In it there were sacks of flour, meal, corn, sugar, salt, and cases of canned food. But most of these things, except perhaps the salt and sugar, would not keep forever, even though I did not use them up. They were already a year old; in five years or so, I estimated, most would be spoiled (though some of the canned stuff might keep longer; I'm not sure).

There were also—in the store—seeds of all kinds: corn, wheat, oats, barley, and most kinds of truck vegetables and fruit—almost everything that will grow here. Also flowers, which I had not even had time to think about. But again, although most of the seeds would germinate after one year, after two years the percentage would decline, and after three or four they would not do well at all.

Even before Mr. Loomis came, I had already been wrestling with the idea that I had to tackle that acre and a half with the shovel. It would have been extremely hard, since it is all covered with a five-year turf. So I was really excited about the tractor, and eager to get started plowing.

I had decided to plant corn as my grain rather than wheat, oats or barley. I would have liked to grow wheat for flour to bake with, but I had no way of processing it—no thresher, no mill. But there was, in the barn, an old hand-cranked machine for making cornmeal and hominy. And, of course, we could eat corn "as is"; the same was true of the beans.

The sun came out—finally—as I started plowing, and was pleasant and warm on my back. Faro had followed

me to the field, looking astonishingly healthy; even his
hair was growing back. He raced in circles around the
tractor, a habit he had picked up years ago when my
father would plow or mow and sometimes flush quail or
partridge hidden in the field. There were none now, of
course, but Faro seemed happy anyway, and so was I. I
felt like singing, but that is hopeless on a tractor; you
can't hear yourself. So instead, as I sometimes do, I began
remembering a poem. I am very fond of poetry, and this
one, one of my favorites, was a sonnet. It began:

> *Oh earth, unhappy planet born to die,*
> *Might I your scribe or your confessor be . . .*

I had thought of that poem many times since the war,
and of myself, by default, as "scribe and confessor." But
now I was neither of those. I was the one, or one of the
two, who might keep it from dying, for a while at least.
When I thought of that, and how my idea of my own
future had been changed in the past week, I could not
stop smiling.

Then, as I plowed, I thought I heard, over the noise of
the tractor, a high squawking sound overhead. I stopped,
turned the engine down to idle, and looked up. There
were crows, sharp and black against the sky, wheeling in
a circle over the field. I counted eleven of them, and I
realized they had remembered the sound of plowing;
they knew there would be seeds to follow. My father

used to call them pests, but I was glad to see them. They were probably the only wild birds left anywhere.

I had half the field plowed by lunchtime. I finished it in the afternoon, and planned to harrow it in the morning, and then seed it. But as it turned out, I had to change my plans.

That night Mr. Loomis's fever went up to 104 degrees.

TEN

June 3, continued

It is because of Mr. Loomis's illness I now have time to write down all that has happened.

I do not dare to leave the house for more than a few minutes at a time. This morning I did. I ran down to the barn to milk the cow, and though I hurried as fast as I could, I was gone about fifteen minutes. When I came back, he was sitting up in bed, his bedclothes on the floor; he was shivering and blue with cold. He was calling me, and had become frightened when I did not answer. The fever makes him afraid to be alone. I got him to lie down again, remade the bed and put some

98

extra blankets on it. There was already some hot water in the kettle, so I filled the hot-water bottle and put it under the blankets. I am afraid he will get pneumonia.

It began last night at dinnertime. He discovered it himself; I did not know at first what was happening. We sat at the table, and he ate about two bites. Then he said, in a strange voice:

"I don't want to eat. I'm not hungry."

I thought perhaps he did not like what I had cooked. It was boiled chicken, gravy, biscuits, and peas.

So I said: "Could I get you something else? Some soup?"

But in the same voice he just said, "No," and pushed his chair back from the table. I noticed then that his eyes looked strange and confused. He went and sat in the chair by the fire.

"The fire is almost out," he said.

"It's turned warm again," I said. "I was letting it die down."

He said: "I'm cold," and got up and went to the bedroom.

I sat at the table continuing to eat (I was hungry after the plowing and other things). Of course, it should have occurred to me immediately what was wrong, but it did not, and a few minutes later he called from the bedroom.

"Ann Burden."

That was the first time he had ever called me by name, and he used both names. I went to the bedroom and found him sitting, looking at the thermometer. He handed it to me and I read it.

"It's started," he said.

Poor Mr. Loomis; his shoulders were slumped and he looked very tired and frail. I realized that in spite of his calmness he was now really afraid. I suppose he had been hoping for a miracle.

"It will be all right," I said. "One hundred four is not so terrible. But you will have to stay in bed, covered up. No wonder you felt cold."

A strange thing had occurred. Though we had both known the fever was coming, and I had dreaded it more than he had (or more than he had seemed to), now that it was there, and he was visibly distressed, my own fear seemed to vanish. I felt calm—almost as if I were the older one. It was as if when he got weaker, I got stronger. I suppose that is why doctors and nurses could last through terrible epidemics.

Doctors and nurses! At least they knew what they were doing. My only training is a one-term course in high school, "Health and Hygiene." I wish they had taught us more. But I tried to think calmly and get organized. He had said the fever would last at least a week, and maybe two. I did not know, during that time, how weak he was likely to get. But at the moment, he was still able to move around, and I thought I should take advantage of that.

The first thing was to keep him warm. I stirred the

fire and added some wood. Then I went upstairs to my parents' bedroom, and from my father's chest of drawers got a pair of flannel pajamas. They were soft and thick; my father used them only on cold winter nights. There were two more pairs in the drawer, and, I was reasonably sure, more still at Mr. Klein's store. The pair I took were red-and-white plaid.

I carried them to his room and put them on his bed.

"You should put these on," I said. "They're warm. And I've built the fire up again. I'm boiling some milk, and when it cools a little, I think you should drink it."

"Now you're sounding like a nurse." He smiled. Either he was less afraid, or he was hiding it better.

"I wish I were," I said. "I don't know enough."

"Poor Ann Burden," he said. "You're going to wish I had never come."

I could not bring myself to tell him what I really wished. How could I tell him about the apple tree, about what I had thought that morning while I picked the flowers and the poke greens? How I felt when I plowed the field? It all seemed remote now and out of place; it made me sad to think about it. So I mentioned something else, something that had been worrying me.

"What I wish—"

"Yes?"

"I wish I had warned you when you . . . went swimming in that creek."

"Could you have? Where were you?"

"Up on the hillside." I still, for some reason, haven't mentioned the cave to him. "I don't know if I could have or not. I could have tried."

"But you didn't know the water was radioactive."

"No. But I knew something was wrong with it."

"I should have known, too. Don't you see? I had two Geiger counters. But I didn't even look. It was my own fault."

But I worried about it anyway, and I still do.

That was last night. He put on the pajamas, and after the milk had boiled and cooled he drank a cup of it, warm; I had boiled the cup, too. I will boil everything pertaining to food from now on, or bake it.

He even consented to take two aspirin tablets. Then he fell asleep. I put the lamp away from the bedside, and turned it down low. I thought I should leave it burning, but I did not want him knocking it over. I cleaned up the dinner dishes, then sat in a chair by the window for about an hour, not doing anything except thinking.

Finally I went to my room and went to sleep. But I got up every hour or so to see how he was, and to check the fire. He slept quietly all night; I wish I could say the same for Faro, who kept dreaming and whining in his sleep. He knows something is wrong.

This morning, as I have said, I went out to the barn to milk, and when I came back I heard him calling before I reached the house. I think he had been having a bad dream just before he woke up, but he did not say anything about it. His eyes looked odd and unfocused, and at first I thought he did not know who I was, he stared at me so hard.

After I got him back in the bed and covered up, he stopped shivering and said: "You went away."

I said: "I was milking the cow."

"While you were gone," he said, "I thought—"

"You thought what?"

"Nothing," he said. "It's the fever. It makes me imagine things." But he would not say what he had imagined. I took his temperature, and it had gone up—it was 105. It looked strange to see the mercury stretched all the way to the wrong end of the thermometer. It only goes to 106 degrees.

He watched me read it. "How is it?" he said.

"Well," I said, "it's a little higher."

"How much higher?"

I told him. "Bad," he said.

"Don't think about it. I'll get you some breakfast."

"I'm not hungry."

"But you must eat anyway."

"I know," he said. "I'll try."

And he did; propped up in bed, he ate most of a boiled egg, some more milk, and a bit of toasted biscuit. When he finished he said: "You know what I would like? Some iced tea. With sugar in it."

I thought he must be joking, but he was not. Poor Mr. Loomis. I said: "I don't have any ice."

103

He said: "I know. We didn't get the generator going in time."

A few minutes later he fell asleep again, and I decided to try, at least. I could not make iced tea, but I could make cool tea, and I thought that what he really wanted was a sweet drink. People with fevers get hungry for odd things—with me it is always chocolate ice cream. There was a tin box half full of tea bags in the pantry— my mother's, not exactly fresh, but they smelled all right. I boiled some water, poured it into a pitcher and put in two bags. After it had steeped awhile, I took out the bags, added quite a lot of sugar and put the pitcher in the basement. It will cool in a few hours, and I will give it to him as a surprise.

But now I face a problem. I have to go to the brook for more water, and sometime soon I am going to have to go to the store, since I am running out of several things, including flour and sugar. But how can I go when he is afraid to be left alone? And I ought to milk the cow again.

This morning I went while he was still asleep. Maybe if I go in broad daylight and tell him while he is awake where I am going, he will be all right. I will have to try that. There is nothing else I can do.

I went, both to the brook and to the store, and it was a bad business, but I could not help it. At least I do not have to go again for a few days. But I can see that I have a very troubled time coming.

I am writing this in the living room; it is night, and I have a lamp lit. Everything is quiet now, at least for the moment.

This is what happened: At about four o'clock this afternoon I knocked on his door and went in. He was asleep (he sleeps about ninety percent of the time now), but woke up and seemed calm enough. I explained that I had to go out, and he did not seem at all bothered or upset; in fact he was surprised that I was worried about it. (*He* had not asked me to stay at the house, of course; it was I who was afraid of going, after what happened this morning—which I think, in fact, he does not even remember.) So I felt a little bit silly, as if I had made too much of it. Still I said:

"I will take the tractor and the cart, so I can go faster and carry more."

"A waste of gas," he said.

I had thought of that, but I decided to do it anyway. It was an emergency, and one that was not likely to happen again, after he had recovered.

Despite his reassurance, I rushed to the barn and hitched the cart to the tractor as quickly as I could; fortunately it is an easy hitch, with just a single six-inch pin to slide through the shaft. The cart is a two-wheeled steel trailer, square, and has a capacity of one ton. When I had it hitched, I put onto it three fifteen-gallon milk cans; I had not used these when I carried water by hand, since they are too heavy. With the tractor the weight did not matter so much, and they would hold enough for two weeks or more. I put the tractor into high gear (it can go about fifteen miles an hour in high) and headed first for the brook.

I filled them (or nearly—about two-thirds full is all I can lift), went on to the store, and loaded up with a lot of food supplies, including canned stuff, dehydrated soup, sugar, flour, cornmeal, dog food, and chicken corn. Before leaving I also refilled the tractor's gas tank from the pump. After all this, including the plowing, it had used only about two-and-a-half gallons, not too bad. As I started back up the road toward the house, I looked at my watch. I had been gone forty minutes.

I was hurrying toward the house, still in high gear, and was perhaps 150 yards away when I saw him. The front door flew open, and Mr. Loomis came out, trying to run but staggering. I could not see his face, but the red-and-white pajamas were unmistakable. He crossed the porch, stopped at the railing, and held on a few seconds, then stumbled down the steps and across the yard toward the tent and the wagon-trunk. Faro ran up, tail wagging, and then backed off, staring at him doubtfully.

By this time I had reached the driveway; I turned in and shut off the motor. Mr Loomis, running in a groping kind of way, as if he could not see well, had not gone to the tent but to the trunk. He opened the end, reached inside, and when his hands came out, to my horror, he was holding the gun, the big carbine. I jumped down and ran toward him, but before I reached him he had fired three shots. He aimed them at the second floor of the house, at my father and mother's bedroom, and I could see puffs of white paint and splintered wood fly off where the bullets hit. The gun made a terrible noise, much louder than the .22.

I shouted—I may have shrieked; I cannot remember—and he turned toward me, swinging the gun around so it was aimed at me. To my own surprise I stayed calm.

"Mr. Loomis," I said, "you're sick. You're dreaming. Put the gun away." His face suddenly looked incredibly distressed and twisted up, as if he might cry, and his eyes were very blurred. But he recognized me and lowered the rifle.

"You went away," he said. Just as before.

"I told you," I said. "I had to go. Don't you remember?"

"I went to sleep," he said. "When I woke up I heard—" He did not want to tell me what he had heard.

"Heard what?"

"I thought I heard . . . somebody in the house. I called you. He was upstairs."

"Who was upstairs?"

But he was being evasive. "Someone moving."

"Mr. Loomis, there was no one in the house. It's the fever again. You *must* stay in bed." It was terrible—

standing outside in pajamas with a fever of 105. I took the gun from his hands and put it back in the trunk. He did not resist, but began to shiver violently, and I saw that both he and the plaid pajamas were soaked with sweat. I got him back into the house and onto the bed. I pulled the blankets over him and went upstairs to get him some dry pajamas.

In my father and mother's room, I saw where the bullets had gone. Fortunately, except for knocking plaster all over the floor, they had done no real damage; they had gone through the wall and almost straight up into the ceiling and hit nothing on the way. I would have to plug the holes up somehow, and sweep the floor.

I got the clean pajamas and gave them to him to change. He can still do that himself; I suppose if he gets so he cannot, I will have to do it. Also I will have to get him a basin to use as a bedpan since he should no longer get up to go to the bathroom.

It was after he had changed pajamas that I realized he had still not quite lost his illusion. I went into his room to get the wet pajamas, to take them to the laundry room. He was lying in the bed with his eyes closed, but when he heard me, he opened them and said, sounding very tired:

"Is he gone?"

I said: "Is who gone?"

"Edward," he said.

"You were dreaming again."

He shook his head, and said: "Yes. I forget. Edward is dead. He couldn't have come all this way."

So it was Edward again. But I am worried. If he is dreaming about Edward, who was, I suppose, a friend of his, why does he want to shoot him?

I think I had better sleep in here, on the sofa. He sleeps very restlessly, muttering and groaning.

I forgot all about giving him his tea, but it will still be good in the morning.

ELEVEN

June 4

Morning.

This is a terrible day.

I do not know how high his fever has gone, because it has reached 106, and beyond that the thermometer does not show. I do not think he can live on very long with such a high temperature.

I remembered from my high-school course that alcohol reduces fever; I found a half bottle of rubbing alcohol in the upstairs medicine closet. Every hour I soak one of my father's handkerchiefs with that and rub his back, chest, arms, neck, and forehead. He tries to draw away—I suppose it must feel like ice—but I think it does help him.

He still sleeps most of the time, and when he wakes up it is because of a dream, a nightmare. Only for a few minutes now and then does he seem to be rational and to recognize me or even see or hear me. The rest of the time he is delirious, and often he is terrified, always of the same thing—he thinks Edward is here and is threatening him with something vague and dreadful. At least it is vague to me.

Still, I am beginning to realize that something bad happened between Mr. Loomis and Edward (I do not know his last name), and that they were not friends at all, but enemies, at least at the end.

Sometimes he acts as if he thinks I am Edward, but more often he stares beyond me, as if I am not there at all; he is looking at someone over my shoulder. It is so real that I turn and look myself, but of course there is no one there. At times he thinks Edward is here in the valley, in the house; at other times Mr. Loomis is back with him near Ithaca, in the laboratory under the mountain. And he says certain things over and over again.

It began this morning. I knocked and went into his room with a glass of the cold tea and a soft-boiled egg I had stirred up in a cup, hoping I could get him to eat a few bites. He was awake, but when he spoke it was not to me; it was to the doorway behind me. He said:

"Stay back, Edward, stay back. It's no use."

I said: "Mr. Loomis, it's me. I've brought you some breakfast."

He rubbed his eyes, and they came into focus. But his voice, when he spoke again, was blurred and tired.

"No breakfast. Too sick."

"Try," I said. "I've brought you some iced tea."

I held out the glass, and to my delight he took it and drank thirstily, finishing half of it without pausing. "Thank you," he said. "That's good." He drank the rest. and closed his eyes. I thought it must be reasonably nourishing, with all the sugar.

"I'll bring more later," I said. "Now try the egg."

But when he opened his eyes again, he was staring at the door. He tried to call out, but his voice was weak:

"Edward?"

I said: "Mr. Loomis, Edward is not here."

"I know," he said. "Where did he go?"

"You mustn't worry about it."

"You don't understand," he said. "He's a thief. He'll steal—" He stopped, as if he had remembered something, and then to my dismay he gave a terrible groan and tried to get out of the bed.

I caught his shoulders and held him back. For a minute he fought quite hard; then he lay still, breathing fast and shallow.

"Poor Mr. Loomis," I said. "Try to understand. You're dreaming. There is no Edward, and nothing to steal."

"The suit," he said, his voice hardly above a whisper. "He'll steal the suit."

The suit. That is what he was worried about, and still is. The safe-suit: for some reason he thinks Edward is trying to steal it.

I said: "Mr. Loomis, the suit is in the wagon, in the trunk. You folded it up and put it there. Can't you remember?"

"In the trunk," he said. "Oh my God. That's where he's gone."

It was obviously the wrong thing for me to have said, because he tried again to get up. I held him down; it was not so hard because he had used up most of his strength the first time. But I am in dread of his getting out of the bed. I am afraid he will fall and hurt himself; more important, I don't know how I would ever get him back in if he does get out. I am sure he is too weak to walk, and I don't know if I can lift and carry him. So I must stay in the room with him, at least until he gets through this nightmare.

The dream is contagious. I suppose it is partly because there are only two of us, and his thoughts affect mine more than they would if I had others to talk to. I sit in the window to write, and I look out and see the wagon-trunk still there, next to the tent as it has always been, and I half expect to see someone—Edward? I don't even know what he looks like!—prowling around it. But there is only Faro lying in the trampled grass by the tent near his dish, waiting to be fed. In a little while I will call him into the house and feed him in here.

No. I have a better idea. When Mr. Loomis calms down a little, as he seems to be doing, I will run out, take Faro's food with me, and get the safe-suit. I will bring it in and put it by the bed where he can see it. I will humor his dream to that extent. It will make him less worried.

Afternoon.

I got the suit and brought it in, but a few minutes later that particular nightmare ended, and he was in another, even worse, perhaps brought on by the sight of the suit. He was back in Ithaca having a most desperate quarrel with Edward. I am glad it was only a dream, because it sounded as if one of them was going to murder the other. As he did before, Mr. Loomis was carrying on a conversation, and I could hear only half of it, but he was hearing both sides. His voice was faint and mumbling; but even so it sounded cold and full of hate, and dangerous . . . I suppose when two men are shut up together in a confined area, the tensions between them grow terrible.

When he began talking, I was sitting by the window and did not hear the first few words. Then it came clearer:

" . . . not for just twenty-four hours, Edward. Not even for twenty-four minutes. If you want to find your

114

family, go ahead. But the suit stays here, and the door stays locked. Don't try to come back."

A pause. He was listening to Edward's reply.

Poor Edward. It was not hard to understand the situation. He and Mr. Loomis were locked up in the underground laboratory, apparently alone. They must have been staying there, working late, perhaps getting some last-minute things done before the people from Washington came, when the bombing began. They had a radio—maybe even television—so they knew what was happening. I suppose they had a telephone, too, but that would not have done much good after the first hour.

Edward was married. He had a wife named Mary and a son named Billy, and he was frantic with worry about them. I don't wonder—I know how he felt. Apparently at first he was afraid to go out—they had real exploding H-bombs in that area, not just drifting fallout. But after the first few days, when things quieted down, he wanted to go and find them, and that is when the fight began.

They knew that the air outside was poisonous with radioactivity, and they had in their laboratory the only suit in the world that would protect against it. One suit, and two people. That was the situation. That is why, in his dream, Mr. Loomis kept reminding Edward that his wife and son were dead; and I suppose Edward had a wild hope that some people might have survived, that they might be alive in a cellar or a shelter.

That was why he wanted to take the suit, even for

twenty-four hours. To find them, if they were alive; and if they were dead, to settle the anguish once and for all. Perhaps to see them one more time, perhaps to bury them. I do not know.

Mr. Loomis was not married; at least I do not think he was, though he had never said anything about it. And he did not want Edward to take the suit. What was the use, if they were dead? In the dream he said:

"How do I know you'll bring it back? Suppose something goes wrong?"

And later:

"Of course they're dead. You heard the radio. There isn't any more Ithaca, Edward. And even if you found them alive—what then?"

A pause.

"You mean you would leave them to bring the suit back? You're lying, Edward."

And again:

"The suit, Edward, the suit. Think about it. It may be the last useful thing anybody ever made. You're not going to waste it on a visit to your dead wife."

Poor Edward. He kept pleading. I found I was wishing Mr. Loomis would lend him the suit, though I could understand why he would not. And I wondered why Edward did not just take it, or at least try. For instance, I thought, Mr. Loomis would have had to sleep some of the time.

And then I learned: that is just what he did do. And

that led to the worst part of the nightmare, for Mr. Loomis, weak as he was, was trying to shout in anger and in dread, and it came out as a horrible, thin whimper. He was also trying again to get up from the bed, to sit, to raise his arms. But he was so weak I did not have to hold him. He could not do it.

I understood now why Edward had been pleading. Because Mr. Loomis was holding, or dreamed he was holding, a gun. I could understand most of what he was saying: he was cursing Edward in terrible language, profanity I will not write down here.

And then he said:

"You're a thief and a liar, Edward, but it's no use. Stand back from the door."

A pause.

"No. I warn you. I will shoot. The suit will stop radiation, but it won't stop bullets."

I remembered. That was the first thing he had said to me when I found him sick in the tent, when he saw my rifle. He was threatening to shoot Edward, as he had in the laboratory, where he had been guarding the door leading out.

In a few more seconds it was over. He gave a desperate groan, a deeper sound than before, and then a series of strangling noises. I thought he must be trying to cry. Then he closed his eyes and lay still, except for his breathing, which was very fast and light, like a small animal that has been running. I tried to take his pulse, but all I could feel was a fluttering, so faint I could not count it.

I wondered if he had really shot Edward, and if so how badly he had injured him. An idea came to me that I did not like, but I decided I must do it anyway. I went to where I had put his suit, folded up on a chair beside his bed. I unfolded it and took it to the window, into the light.

What I had feared was true. There were three holes, spaced about two inches apart, across the middle of the chest. They had been patched—that is, new plastic had been welded over them so that they were airtight—but from the inside you could see that they were bullet holes, round and quite large. If Edward was inside the suit when they were fired, then he had certainly been killed.

Night.

It is about ten o'clock. I am in the bedroom, sitting by the window with the lamp. His dreams seem to be over; he is peaceful, but I do not know if he will live through the night. His hands and feet are ice-cold; his breathing is faint, almost undetectable. I have not tried taking his temperature again. It would only disturb him, and would do no good. There is nothing more I can do for him.

I realized that late this afternoon. It is an empty, despairing feeling. There is not even any use in my staying with him continuously, since he can no longer get out of the bed, or even fall out. His hands are very cold. I got another blanket when I first noticed how really bad he is, and the hot-water bottle, and I lifted his head on my arm and tried to get him to drink more of the tea. He may have swallowed a little; I could not be sure. He did not open his eyes. His face is pale blue, his eyelids almost purple, and translucent.

Then I had a thought of something that might do him some good. I checked his bedroom one more time, and then I went out and closed the door, left the house and walked to the church, taking the Bible with me. I do not want to make it sound as if I am extremely religious, but I did not know what else to do, so I thought I might pray. I said I thought it might do him some good; maybe what I really thought was that it might do me some good. I cannot be sure. But I knew he needed help, and so did I.

The sun was setting, and it was pretty again, but I could not admire it. I felt too bad. Faro came with me, and I was glad at least to see him. When I got to the church, he wanted to come in with me, and I let him, but made him lie still.

The inside of the church is painted white, though the paint has faded somewhat, and in the late evening light it looked pale gray. It is very small, a single square room; there are seven pews, but only two of them have backs; the others are really just benches. There are two narrow windows behind the altar (there is no pulpit, but just a high oblong stand to read from), and two more set in the side walls, also narrow, so that it is always dim inside, and quiet.

I sat in the front pew, where the light is best, and read the Bible for half an hour, and I prayed for Mr. Loomis. I prayed just for him to live through the night. Even though he may be a murderer, I do not want him to die.

TWELVE

June 5

Morning.

He has lived through the night.

Once I was sure he had died. I slept on the sofa in the living room, and all night he did not make a sound. I could not really sleep for any length of time, but dozed now and then, and in between I would go in and see how he was. About two in the morning I went in, listened for his breathing, and did not hear it. I felt so frightened I thought my own heart was going to stop. I said a prayer and crept closer. Finally, from about a foot away, I did hear it, terribly faint and fast. Each time after that it was the same, but it did not stop. I kept the fire going and changed the hot-water bottle every hour, putting it next to his feet. They are so cold I am sure they are not getting any circulation.

Morning finally came, and I fixed myself some breakfast and coffee; though I have no appetite I must eat. I also went and milked the cow; I am afraid of her going dry immediately if I neglect that much more, since the calf is beginning to graze. When I came back, the room was light, and I looked at him. He was so pale it was frightening. I did not try to take his temperature, but I did count his respiration. He was breathing almost fifty times a minute; I recall from my school course that normal is about sixteen. His lips looked puffy, gray, and cracked, and they felt dry as cardboard. I got a clean cloth and soaked it in water, then held it to his lips and moistened them, squeezing it gently so that some of the water might trickle into his mouth. I did not dare try to give him water from a glass, for fear he might strangle. I washed his face, which was cold and sticky.

I fed Faro and walked to the church again. This time I knew it was mostly for my own benefit; I was so worried I could not think clearly; I felt dizzy and ill, I suppose partly because I had had next to no sleep. But there was nothing to be gained by sitting in the house and watching. Either he was going to die or he was not. My being there would make no difference.

Anyway, I was worried not just about whether he

would live, but about what had happened in the laboratory—what I had *heard* happening in the laboratory—because that is what I had done, just as surely as if it were a recording. And that was the reason I needed to be able to think clearly.

Faro bolted his breakfast and caught up with me. We went into the church together. I was just realizing that I had forgotten the Bible, and was considering whether I should go back for it, when I noticed that he had come to a point and was inching along the church floor toward the altar. I could see nothing there, and it gave me an eerie feeling. In the stillness, for a second, I thought he might be stalking a spirit or an angel.

I motioned him to lie still, went forward myself, rather fearfully, and then I saw it: a small, rumpled black thing—a baby crow, no bigger than a sparrow, its furry down just beginning to sprout feathers that would be wings and a tail. It fluttered away from me when I came near, but it could not get itself off the floor. Where had it come from? And how had it gotten into the church? I looked up, and above me rose the square opening that formed the inside of the steeple, actually more like a high cupola. Near the top there was a crisscross wooden framework of two-by-fours built (we had been told) to support a church bell, though no bell had ever been brought here. On one side of this, just inside the eaves of the roof (where I had noticed some boards were missing) I saw a rather untidy collection of sticks, leaves, and straw, a nest. A pair of crows had built there, and one of the babies had fallen out.

I watched it and it watched me, with very lively small black eyes. I moved a step closer; it fluttered a step farther away, until finally it was against the wall behind the altar. Then it just gave up and sat there.

I had found baby birds before, of course. All of us had, and my father had told us that we should always leave them where they were, since the parent birds were usually watching from a nearby tree and would rescue the baby if we stayed away. He was right. I have seen them do it. But I did not think it likely that the adult crows would venture down the steeple into the church, or that they would even realize where the baby had fallen.

So I picked it up, holding it as gently as I could in both hands. It did not struggle, but sat quite trustingly. I was tempted to take it home and feed it, but realized that I had enough to think about without a pet to take care of. Also, as soon as I carried it outside I heard a raucous sound, looked up, and there were two big crows flapping overhead. One of them came to rest on the steeple, so I knew they must be the parents and had seen what I held in my hands. I set the baby down in the grass where they could not miss finding it, and when I had retreated up the road a short way (calling Faro with me—he was intensely interested in the whole procedure), I saw that they had already flown down to it. I never heard of crows nesting in a steeple before, but I suppose they change their habits when there are no other birds around.

As I walked back to the house, I decided it might be a good omen. I am a little superstitious, and have always thought that birds bring good luck; when I wake up in the morning, look out the window, and see a bird the first thing—especially if it is close up, and looking toward me—I feel as if it is a symbol, and that something good will happen that day. I suppose that is because when I was about four and first heard about prayers, I was told that they flew up to heaven. So I thought of them as rather like birds, with wings, flying upward.

This one, of course, flew (fell!) downward from above, the wrong direction for a prayer. Still it made me feel a bit more cheerful as I walked back to the house, even when I remembered that I had forgotten to say any prayer at all.

Evening.

He is still the same. I do not know what keeps him alive. I do not dare try to move him; I have the feeling that the least disturbance, even a loud noise, might snap the thread. So I still have not changed the bed, though it is soiled.

When I came back from the church, I spoke to him, very softly, I just told him I was there. He did not wake up, nor even flicker his eyelids. Yet I had a feeling he heard me, even if unconsciously, and that it was good for him to know someone was there.

In fact, I was so convinced of this that I decided to read to him, quietly, sitting by his bed so he would sense where I was. I thought of the Bible, but in the end decided poetry might be more soothing, so I brought an anthology from my room and read Gray's "Elegy Written in a Country Churchyard." It is sad, but I like it. I realized it was about death, but I was sure he could not understand the words at all; I only hoped he might hear the sound.

Again, I am not too sure for whose benefit I was really doing it. Reading the poem certainly made me feel less worried and confused. I thought that later I might also play the piano, something quiet, using the soft pedal. It is, after all, in the next room, and he did like it when I played before.

After I finished Gray's "Elegy" I sat in the chair thinking about him and Edward.

I suppose I have to accept the idea that Mr. Loomis shot Edward and killed him, and that is a terrible thought, because he is the only other human being I am ever likely to know.

Of course I do not know for sure that he did it. But from what he said in his dream, and from the holes in the suit, I cannot help believing he did. From what he said, too, I cannot be sure how wrong it was. In a way, it was self-defense. If Edward had taken the suit, and left, and never come back, he would, in effect, have doomed Mr.

Loomis to stay in the laboratory—perhaps forever—*probably* forever. There he would eventually have run out of food, or water or air, and died. So in a way Edward was, when he tried to steal the suit, threatening to kill him.

Also, Mr. Loomis may have been concerned about more than just staying alive. In his dream he said that the suit was too important to waste. He called it "the last useful thing." He may have been thinking not just of himself, but of human survival. At that time he surely still believed that there might be groups of people alive in shelters—underground Air Force bases, and so on—and the suit, the only one of its kind, might be the only way to contact them. It *was* too important to waste. If he was thinking about that, and if Edward would not consider it, if Edward was being selfish and foolish, then Edward was wrong.

In a way it depends on what Edward was like. If he was honest and sensible and really meant to return the suit, and would have returned it, then maybe Mr. Loomis should have let him borrow it. Except, of course, as he said—suppose something went wrong? But if Edward was just being thoughtless and trying to sneak away, then I cannot blame Mr. Loomis so much.

But suppose, on the other hand, Mr. Loomis was trying to keep the suit for himself? Suppose he meant to take it, when the time came, and strike out on his own, hoping to find civilization surviving somewhere? That is what he finally did.

So in a way it also depends on knowing what Mr. Loomis was like—*is* like. And it is true that I really do not know that, not yet.

I keep wondering. If he lives and becomes conscious again—should I ask him about it? He obviously did not want to tell what happened, since in his own story of the laboratory, and the suit, and his trip to Chicago he never mentioned Edward at all. And yet it would be hard, with only two of us, for me to know this secret and try to hide it.

I will have to decide.

June 6

This morning I went to church again. I had just about given up hope. He had lain absolutely motionless, with no flicker of life except the faintest of breathing, for more than thirty-two hours. I began to feel as if I were alone again after all. It was hard to think of him as a person; the belief that he could talk and think began to slip away. Yet I did not want to give up; I felt that if I did, he would, too. That is why I went to church.

The day was cloudy, with a fresh, wet smell in the air. It had rained a little during the night, and would rain again. When Faro and I reached the church, Faro ran and sniffed around in the grass where I had left the bird, but it was gone. I am sure the parents got it back into the nest.

This time I remembered to take the Bible with me, and also to say a prayer.

On the way back I picked some flowers, some wild roses that grow beside the road, and at home I put them in a vase and took them to his room. The apple blossoms had wilted and fallen off. He cannot see them, of course. Again for my benefit.

Then I sat by his bed and counted his respiration as well as I could. I did it over three times, and as far as I could tell it had fallen from fifty to about thirty. It seemed also a little deeper.

I am not sure whether that is a good sign or not, but it may be.

I played the piano for half an hour, hoping it would penetrate to wherever he was.

THIRTEEN

June 7

He is definitely better.

He still does not wake up, but his respiration is down to eighteen per minute, almost normal, and his color has come up from blue to white. And he *looks* better. I have not yet taken his temperature but I can tell, from touching his forehead and then my own, that although it is still high, it is not as high as it was.

Taking advantage of this improvement (which may, I know, be only temporary) I changed his sheets, blankets, pillowcase, and pajamas. To get the old sheets off and the clean ones on, I had to roll him from one side of the bed to the other (this was one thing they had taught in the hygiene course), and I did that very cautiously; it did not seem to harm him, however, nor affect his breathing.

Altogether, it was quite a messy job. I have a big wash to do, and I know now that I was not cut out to be a nurse. I did consider it at one time; from a distance it seemed like a good profession. I would be helping people who needed help, and if I was trained, I would get paid for doing it. But I had decided on teaching instead; it is also a job of helping people, though perhaps not as much as nursing.

It is still hard for me to realize, even after all this time, that I am not going to *be* anything, not ever have a job or go anywhere or do anything except what I do here. I had chosen teaching because I liked specifically the idea of teaching English. I like books and reading more than anything else. My plan was, as I taught, also to study, to take graduate courses in English literature and possibly writing.

That whole idea is over now; there are no more schools and there is no one to teach. I know that; yet I keep thinking about it. Another part of my plan was to live at home, save money, and spend my entire first year's salary on books. I have so few that I have read them all twenty times or more.

Thinking about that has set me to wondering. A lot of the books I would like to buy—would *have* liked to buy—are in the Ogdentown Public Library. There is also a gift shop in Ogdentown, which has a small bookstore in it. For that matter, there are some pretty big houses there that probably have books that nobody else is ever going to read. What I wonder is, could I bring some of them here?

I am thinking of the safe-suit of course. Having traveled all this way, Mr. Loomis could easily—I should think—make a trip to Ogdentown to get some books.

But would they be dangerous to bring into the valley? Or would it be possible to set them out somewhere—up the hillside, with a cover over them to keep the rain off—until they lost their radioactivity? I think we could test them (like the creek) once a week with the Geiger counter. I don't know enough about that, but Mr. Loomis would. Though he might not be too interested, being, apparently, not much of a reader.

Thinking about this I get really excited. Yet I am not sure. I thought: if it could be done, if the books would become safe to handle, and Mr. Loomis did not want to go, *I* could go. That is, if he would lend me the safe-suit.

And that thought brought me back to Edward, with a jolt.

June 8

He opened his eyes this morning, but they were blank and unfocused, the eyes of a newborn animal. He was

132

not seeing anything at all.

He also seemed to be trying to speak, or make a noise, but all that came out was a croak. I guessed he was asking for water. I got some and fed it to him with a spoon. He wanted it all right; I gave him half a glass and then stopped, afraid he would get sick if he drank too much too quickly. The best thing was that he could swallow it quite well, though some did run out the corners of his mouth and down his chin.

I knew he was not really conscious. But it was progress, and I felt better. A little later I also took his temperature. I had to sit and hold both the thermometer and his chin (which has grown whiskery), but it worked. He has 103—*much* better.

But he is skin and bones. Now that he could swallow, at least liquids, food seemed the next thing to work on. I thought about the most nourishing liquids I could concoct. Soup, of course. But even better, I decided, boiled custard. I made some—milk, egg yolks, sugar, salt. While I waited for the milk to boil, I wished again for the stove.

And I thought—well, why not. I had the tractor now.

When I had dismantled the stove, I planned to haul it, piece by piece, on the small (and rather rickety old) hand truck. I had not even thought about it since I—we—got the tractor running. With the tractor cart I could move the whole thing in a matter of minutes. And it would not take long to reassemble it in the kitchen; I knew exactly where I wanted it to stand.

So, while I waited for the custard to cool, I ran to the barn, backed the tractor and cart to the loading platform and lowered the tailgate. The cart and the platform are almost exactly the same height—not by accident; my father built a sort of earth-ramp leading up to the barn just for that purpose.

I had already put the firebox, the heaviest part, on its masonite sled, so with some tugging I soon had it aboard the cart. The other parts I simply carried on.

Unloading at the back porch of the house was equally easy. It was about six inches lower than the cart, so I unchained the tailgate and used it as a gangplank. Getting the firebox over the doorsill was a small problem, but I remembered a trick of my mother's: I rubbed the sill with very soapy water, and the masonite slid over easily.

Reassembling the stove was harder than I had thought it would be. Some of the bolts did not want to slip through their holes; also I put the grate on backward the first time and had to take it off again. I worked on the project all afternoon, taking time out now and then to check on Mr. Loomis (quite a lot of hand-washing each time).

When his custard was cool enough, I tried feeding it to him with a spoon, a sip at a time. Again he did not wake up, nor, this time, even open his eyes. But he did swallow, gulping each spoonful with an effort. Swallowing seems to be a reflex, an instinct not requiring thought, and I am glad of that. Still I gave him only about two ounces at the first feeding. I wanted to be sure he could digest it.

The stove is finished. It needs only two lengths of straight stovepipe and an elbow, which I will get from Mr. Klein's store, to connect it to the kitchen chimney. Then I will polish it. It is black with nickel trim, and will look beautiful. I am proud of it—especially the oven—and of myself; it is like getting a Christmas present.

FOURTEEN

A week has passed, one of the best of weeks.

Today is my birthday. I am sixteen, and for dinner we had a roast chicken and a cake, both cooked in my new oven. I will not say it is the first cake I ever baked; I have done it before, but always under my mother's supervision. So I will say it is the first I have baked alone, and the first in this oven, and it came out perfect. I made a white cream frosting, and it was perfect, too.

We were celebrating not only my birthday, but Mr. Loomis's recovery, which has been astonishing, though it is still not complete. He still cannot walk; his legs are weak and buckle under him. As I suspected, they were not getting proper circulation. I think they will be all right eventually, but it is slow.

So we had the birthday dinner on a folding card table, which I set beside his bed. I put a white linen cloth on it and set it with the good china; I even polished the silver, and this time I remembered to get candles (not birthday-cake candles, however; I couldn't find any in Mr. Klein's store).

The best thing about getting it ready was that Mr. Loomis slept through the preparations, and then woke up just at the right time. The table was all set, and the candles were shining on the silver. He opened his eyes, looked at it, closed them and opened them again. He said: "It seems like a miracle." And in a way it really did, when I considered that a week ago he was nearly dead, and I had almost given up hope. But I think he was talking about the table.

His recovery had already begun the day I began feeding him, though I was not sure of it at the time. I felt surer the next day, late in the afternoon, when he finally woke up. I had just walked into the room, and apparently he heard me; his eyes opened, focused, and I could tell he saw me. To my amazement, he spoke, very faintly, and the first thing he said was:

"You played the piano."

I wanted to hug him, but instead I sat down in the chair by the bed. I said: "Yes. I didn't know if you could hear."

"I heard. It faded away . . ." His eyes closed, and he

did not finish the sentence. He was asleep again already.

It was not much, and yet it seemed momentous. He could see, he could talk again! I let him sleep for half an hour; then I got some soup I had made and sat down to feed it to him as I had been doing with the custard. He woke up again immediately. He did not talk anymore at first, but swallowed the soup spoon by spoon—I can even say hungrily, because he did seem to like it. I had brought a cupful, and he ate it all. Then he said:

"I was . . . away." His voice was a little stronger. "I heard you playing . . . so faint. I tried to listen . . ." He had lost his breath and he stopped. "It faded . . . but I tried, and it came back . . ."

I said: "You're too weak to talk. Don't try. But I'm glad you heard it." Poor Mr. Loomis. I think he was saying that my playing had helped him. I wondered if he had heard my reading, too.

He had. The next day he seemed twice as strong. His temperature was only 101, and I had not even done the alcohol rub. He could move a little, though not enough to feed himself. And he kept his eyes open longer, looking at things in the room. When he spoke again, he was not so vague and breathless; but he was still remembering back to the bad days, as before.

"I thought I was a long way from—from everything. Someplace cold. Floating away. It was hard to breathe. But I heard you talking, and then the floating stopped as long as I listened. And the same with the music."

"You're much better now."

"I know. Not so cold anymore."

I fed him more of the custard and the soup, about every two hours, and he seemed to be hungrier each time. In fact, his appetite became very good, and on the third day I switched to solid food. He was making up, of course, for all the days he had eaten nothing. I would guess he had lost fifteen pounds or more.

On the fourth day, another milestone. I went in with his lunch, prepared to feed it to him as before. He was on his side, propped up on one elbow, and I noticed that the color in his face was much better. He said:

"If you'll help me up, I think I can do it myself."

"Do what?"

"Eat."

I hesitated and he said, quite urgently: "Let me try, at least."

So I got some more pillows and put an arm under his shoulders to help him up. He sat with the lunch in his lap and fed himself; he was rather shaky but was obviously determined to do it, and seemed to feel satisfied with himself when he did. I suppose he had felt like a baby, being spoon-fed.

My worry over him grew less each day, and as always with worries (mine at least), when a big one fades away, the smaller ones start creeping in. I went out to the garden I had been neglecting—I had scarcely looked at it for ten days—and the field I had plowed but never planted. They are, as I said, smaller worries, but real ones. We can live through next winter on what is in the store, and so can the cows and the chickens. But there is a danger point beyond that, because the seeds I have are already two years old, and next year they will be three, and each year fewer of them will germinate. So I really needed to get some in the ground, if only to harvest the new seeds.

I regarded this worry as entirely my own, and of course did not intend to say anything to Mr. Loomis about it. I walked through the rows of the garden and saw that everything had come up; the earth had grown somewhat too hard and caked, but that had done no damage yet. I could fix it quickly with a hoe and a hand cultivator—both were leaning against the fence near the gate where I had left them. On the whole I was satisfied. Everything was a month late, which meant the peas would not do much if it turned hot—not many to eat, but surely enough for seeds next spring. We would have lettuce, radishes and mustard greens starting in two more weeks. Even the potatoes had small but healthy looking green vines coming.

I walked down to the field. It still lay in furrows, looking rather desolate, and a few weeds had come up. I had not yet harrowed it, however, and that would take care of those. The important thing was to get the corn planted; it, at least, would do all right, though it would not ripen until late September or October. That would be in plenty of time for winter feed for the cows and chickens; and I could cut some off and can it, and also grind cornmeal. Mainly, I would have plenty of new seed for next year.

I am not too sure about the soybeans. I have never grown them and cannot remember when my father used to plant them. I think they should have been sown earlier. Still I will try—again, I should get at least a seed crop.

All of these were important problems, serious, but I could solve them if I got to work quickly. And, as I said, I had not intended even to mention them to Mr. Loomis. But on the fifth day he did two surprising things, one connected with the plowing and planting, the other not.

The first one I could almost call a scolding.

When I brought him his breakfast tray, he said: "Is the tractor still running?"

"Well," I said, "it is, though I haven't used it much."

"How is the planting? Has the garden come up? And the corn?"

His tone was nervous, almost suspicious. I thought I had heard it before—then I remembered—it was the voice he had used with Edward. I confessed.

"The garden is all right. It needs hoeing. But the corn . . ."

"Yes?" Very impatiently.

"I haven't planted it yet. Nor the beans."

At that he acted very disturbed. He raised himself on

his elbow—in fact he almost sat up. He was much stronger.

"Not planted it? Why not?"

"You were so sick," I said. "I was too worried—"

He interrupted. "What has that to do with planting?"

"When your fever was high and you were delirious, I didn't dare leave. I didn't want—"

"You mean you never left the house?"

"Not at first. Except a few minutes to milk the cow."

Then I made a mistake.

I said: "In the end, I did go to the church."

"To *church*?" He sounded as if he could not believe it. "To *church*!" He lay back in the bed. "How long did that take?"

I said: "I'm not sure. I went three times." I realized that I should not have mentioned it at all. It seemed to irritate him so.

"Three times to church, and the field not planted."

I wanted to explain how I had felt, how important it had seemed when I thought he was dying, but I realized that would only make him more upset.

So instead I said: "It's not really so bad. We often planted corn this late—even in July. It does very well."

"When does the frost begin?" He sounded skeptical.

"Never until November. And the corn will be ready in October—maybe September."

"If you plant it now."

I said: "I was planning to start today. I went yester-

142

day and looked at the field. I have to run the harrow over it first."

"How long does that take?"

"Half a day. I can plant some this afternoon. Maybe all of it."

He seemed mollified. In a way, he even tried to explain. "I worry about food. I even dream about it."

Yet I was startled. He had sounded annoyed and did not understand why I had gone to church and how much I had wanted him to live. I might still try to explain, but later. After the planting was done, it would not be such a sore subject.

But there was more to it than that, when I got to thinking about it. I had been regarding the field, the tractor—the *valley*—and the planting and garden, all as things of mine, to do or to worry about. But now he had begun thinking about them as his, too. I thought I could figure out why. It was because, all of the time until now, he had been sick. It was when he was first sick that I had let him know I was here. And now, for the first time, that was over. He was not completely recovered yet, but he had realized that he was going to be, that he was going to live. That was the change. And so he considered the valley as much his as mine. I would have to get used to the idea.

The other thing he did was not so serious. In fact, it would have seemed funny except that it was rather pathetic.

I spent the morning running the harrow. Even though the soil had set for two weeks—which it is not supposed to do—it broke up easily, and I watched the ugly corkscrew hummocks of the plow change into smooth, narrow ridges, looking the way a field ought to look. Faro bounded around the tractor, his feet stirring up small sprays of dirt with each bound. He knows not to get near the wheels.

In the afternoon I planted, getting the corn about three-fourths done before it was time to go in and start the supper. As I planted, I began thinking about the fact that my birthday was coming in two days.

That made the stove even more of a joy than it had been, because as I got the fire going I realized that I could have a real birthday cake, layers and all. I was just starting to cook when I heard a loud *thud* from Mr. Loomis's bedroom, and then a series of smaller thumping noises. It sounded like a struggle going on.

And so it was—a solitary one. I ran to the bedroom door and saw Mr. Loomis: he was on the floor, sprawled in an awkward heap, holding to the bed and trying to get up.

I ran to him. "Did you fall?"

He said: "Not exactly. I was stupid. I tried to get up." He raised himself to his knees and then, with a really painful effort, tried to get back on the bed. He almost succeeded, but at the very end he rested his weight on his legs and his knees buckled in a rubbery way just like a comedian I once saw trying to act drunk. He fell to the floor again.

I said: "Let me help you up."

"No," he said, quite fiercely. "I can do it. Just don't stand and watch." He felt foolish—I could understand that—so I went and stood outside the door. In a minute I heard him try again, and that time I heard the bed creak as he pulled himself back onto it. I went back to the kitchen and cooked the dinner. When I took him his tray he seemed cheerful enough. He did not mention the incident at all, but asked me if I could bring him the following things: some pencils, plain white paper, a ruler, a protractor, and a drawing compass.

As it happened, I had them all in my desk upstairs, left over from geometry. I brought them to him after dinner, and then began planning my birthday cake.

FIFTEEN

June 22

During the week since my birthday he has learned to walk again. But only very weakly, while holding on to something.

The first three days he tried and failed, as he had before. He was secretive about it; I do not know exactly why. Probably because he felt foolish when I saw him after he fell. Or maybe he wanted to surprise me. But I heard him from the kitchen: the thud as his feet reached the floor and the creak of the bed as he pulled himself back. He may also have done this other times when I was outside working. I think what he was actually doing was exercising his legs—putting as much weight on them as he could, a bit more each time.

And on the fourth day he succeeded—again, entirely in private. In the kitchen (getting lunch) I heard the same thud as before, but then, quite unmistakably, the sound of a footstep, then another and a third, very slow and cautious. I felt like running in and applauding! But I decided if he wanted my approval he would have called me. He obviously feels that it is his problem and he is going to solve it himself.

However, that left me as an eavesdropper—apparently he did not realize the sound could be heard in the kitchen—and, not wanting to feel sneaky, I thought I should let him know. I had settled into the custom of eating my meals (except breakfast) on the card table by his bed. So when I brought the tray in, I took my own food off, gave him his, and said:

"I thought I heard you walking."

He was by this time back in the bed, but sitting up and studying a diagram he had drawn on one of his pieces of paper. He had been making drawings steadily during the past week: he was designing the water-powered generator.

He looked up without expression and said: "It's something I have to do."

He did not even seem interested, but looked back at his diagram and added: "I wish I had a book. These magazines don't tell enough." He had the copies of *The*

Farm Mechanic beside him on the bed.

"What kind of book?"

"Engineering. Physics. Electricity. I guess it would be several books. Also a good encyclopedia. You don't have one?"

"No. But I know where there is one. In the library in Ogdentown."

"Ogdentown?"

"You must have passed through it when you came here. The library is the gray stone building on Court Street."

"I passed through many towns. Hundreds."

"Well, Ogdentown must have been the last one."

"How far from here?"

To my joy, it sounded as if he was going to suggest going for books.

"Not far," I said. "Only over the second ridge."

"How many *miles*?"

"Well, about twenty. A little over twenty." (Actually it is closer to twenty-five.)

There was a pause. He ate several bites of his lunch and did not say any more.

So I asked: "If we brought books from there—brought them here—would they be dangerous? Radioactive?"

"Yes."

"For how long? Permanently?"

"No. They'd cool off eventually. Maybe six months,

148

maybe more—maybe less. It depends partly on size."

I said: "So long?"

"That wouldn't matter too much. I could wear the suit and go and copy out what I need—gear ratios, things like that."

"But I was hoping to read them. Still, I suppose I could wait six months."

"You wouldn't enjoy reading technical books."

"They have other books in the library. They have whole sets of Shakespeare, Dickens, Hardy. And poetry."

As I suspected, he was not too interested in that. He ate some more and then said: "It doesn't matter anyhow—right now at least. I can't walk that far. When I can—"

And then, because I had been thinking about it so hard, I said the wrong thing again.

"But I can. If you'd lend me the suit, I could go."

I could hardly believe how annoyed that made him. I should have known, I guess, having heard him dreaming when he was sick, and the way he talked to Edward.

"No," he said, his voice very quiet, but angry and hard. "You could *not* go. Understand that. Keep away from the suit. Never touch it."

I started to remind him that I had already touched it. But I caught myself in time. I realized that he probably did not remember, since he had been sick and delirious at the time. We ate on in rather tense silence, I wondering why he was still so extremely sensitive about the suit, when he had found a place where he could stay. It occurred to me that maybe he was afraid I would see the bullet holes. Yet that seemed unlikely since I had never talked to him about his dreams—how would I know what the patches were?

His lunch finished (his appetite was not impaired!) he went on, sounding a little less unfriendly. In fact, he tried to smile, but still it was rather like a lecture.

"You must understand," he said, "that except for ourselves, that suit is the most important thing in the world. There is no other, and no way now of making another. Except for this valley the rest of the world, as far as we know, is dangerous and uninhabitable. I don't know how long it's going to be that way—maybe forever.

"But as long as it is, the suit is the only way to go out there and stay alive. The idea of taking it to get some novels—it's too foolish to consider. If you took it out and something went wrong, I could never get it back. I couldn't go out after it, couldn't even try. It would be lost forever."

That is what Edward had been up against—even some of the words were the same. Yet I could not argue. After all, it was his suit. And also, of course, what he said was true. I could survive without novels.

Still, it had been a pleasant thing to think about; I had

even let my imagination run to the point of making several trips, building up a real home library. So, though I can see that it is not too practical, especially from Mr. Loomis's point of view, I will continue to hope that when he can walk better, if he goes to get technical books he may slip in at least one or two books for me to read. That may be a less offensive idea.

At the time, however, I changed the subject to something less controversial. I asked him: "How far did you walk?"

"Four steps, holding on to the bed. This morning, three steps."

"As soon as you can do a little more, I could fix a chair for you outside on the front porch. Then you could get out of this room for a while."

"I had thought of that. And on the back porch, too, where I can see the planting."

"The corn is beginning to come up," I said. "In a few more days I'll have to thin it. The peas and beans are in, but not up yet."

"How about beets? And wheat?"

"Well, I had not planned—"

"We must plan. Not just for next year, but beyond. Beets make sugar. Wheat makes flour."

I had started to say that since I could only plant and cultivate so much, I had not included beets—and quite a few other things, like pumpkins, turnips, squash, and so on. There were seeds for all of them in the store. But when I had made my plans, I had not counted on the tractor.

"I know what you're thinking," he said. "There's plenty of sugar in the store. I saw that. And it keeps. But when it's gone—what then? You see, that's foolish and shortsighted." His voice had grown edgy again.

He went on: "I've been lying in the bed for a long time now, with nothing to do but think. And I realized that we've got to plan as if this valley is the whole world, and we are starting a colony, one that will last permanently."

It was the same thought, or nearly the same, as the one I had had when I was plowing. Yet his saying it, or the way he said it, made me feel uneasy. I am not sure why.

As I was taking the tray out, he said another thing: "When you go to your church, if you want something to pray for, pray for that bull calf."

I said: "I don't understand." The calf seemed perfectly healthy.

He said: "When the gasoline is gone, cattle can pull the plow."

It was true that some of the Amish, being slow to change their ways, used to plow with mules or oxen. I remember seeing them when I was small. There was even an old wood and leather harness hanging on the wall of our own barn, thought I had never seen it used.

What he meant was that we needed to breed more

cattle, and I had planned that, at least, from the beginning.

He asked me to bring him a new razor and blades
from the store. I did, and he has shaved his whiskers off
again. It makes him look healthier.

SIXTEEN

June 24

In these few days my uneasiness has grown worse.

At Mr. Loomis's urging, I planted wheat and beets. I put the beets, two long rows of them, in the same field with the corn, next to the soybeans. If the crop is good, we will have more beets than we can eat; but the object is to harvest the seed. If I do that each year, then someday, when we need them for sugar, we will have them. I admit that it is a sensible idea.

There was not room for the wheat in that field, so I planted it—about a half acre—in the far field beyond the pond. This means that there will be a little less pasture, but it doesn't matter, since after I cut what I need for seed—a few bushels should be enough—the cows can eat the rest. The chickens can eat it, too, though they like corn better.

I explained to Mr. Loomis why I had not planned to grow wheat—that is, that I had no way to mill it for flour.

"That's not important," he said. "When I get well enough, when I can walk farther, we can learn how to mill it. The important thing is not to let the species die out."

None of that had anything to do with my feeling uneasy. It was caused by something else.

As I had said I would, I put a chair for him out on the front porch—a small upholstered armchair I got from my parents' bedroom. It also has a matching footstool, and I brought that down, too, along with a pillow and a blanket. It was really quite comfortable (I tried it).

As he requested, I also put a chair on the back porch; there is not enough room there for a footstool, so it is not quite as nice. However, yesterday morning when I asked him he said the back porch was where he wanted to sit.

It was the first time since his sickness that he had ventured out of his room, but he did quite well. I had remembered, searched for, and found in the front coat closet something I had forgotten: a cane my father once used when he had a sprained ankle. With that, and leaning heavily on my shoulder, he made it to the porch and into the chair. His knees still buckle under him, and he cannot lift his feet properly, but he does manage to move.

He sat in the chair all morning—rather like an over-seer—watching while I plowed, harrowed and then planted the two rows of beets. After lunch he slept in his room while I started on the wheat field. When the sun began moving over the hill, I came back to the house; he was awake and wanted to go out again, this time to the front porch. So I helped him to the chair, got his feet on the footstool, and fixed the blanket. Then I went inside to start the dinner.

What happened after that is, I suppose, partly my own fault. Having put the food in the oven and the kettle on to boil, I got a straight chair from the dining room, took it out on the porch and sat down beside him. I had a reason for doing this, besides just wanting to rest a few minutes. It was a feeling that had been growing on me, and bothering me more each day since he first began to recover. I had realized that I did not know him at all. When he had first come, I had been so excited and apprehensive about the presence of *any* other person that I did not think too much about *who* Mr. Loomis was; he had seemed attractive and friendly. But since his recovery, I had felt that I did not understand him at all.

He had given me only the barest account of how he had gone to work in the laboratory on the plastic and the safe-suit, and about the trip he had made to the underground Air Force headquarters. I had learned from his nightmares about his fight with Edward. But that was all I knew. He had never talked about himself at all. If possible, he was even more reserved now than he had been before his illness. Nor did he seem to have any curiosity or interest in me, except once he had seemed to like my playing the piano.

I had a theory about it, more than one really. I thought the murder of Edward, the months alone in the laboratory, the long desperate walks, also alone, through the dead countryside—all that had been so horrible and deadening it had blotted out everything else in his mind. When he thought back, that was what popped up, so he did not think back, nor talk about the past. But beyond that, his sickness and at the end the high temperature may have done something to him; the temperature might even have changed parts of his mind. It was not impossible, I thought. Yet, whatever the cause, I did not believe we could go on forever as strangers, knowing as little about each other.

I did not want to discuss the thing about Edward (I decided probably not ever) nor the laboratory, but wanted to get him talking about the times before that I sat down beside him, but I did not know how to do it. In books and movies they say, "Let's talk about you," or, "Tell me all about yourself"—but that is when they first meet, and seems trite anyway.

Remembering that he had liked my playing music, I asked:

"When you were young, did somebody in your family play the piano?"

He said: "No. We didn't have a piano."

"Were you poor?"

"Yes. I had a cousin I used to visit. They had a piano, and his mother played it. I liked to listen to that."

"Where was that?"

"A town in New York. Nyack."

He did not elaborate, and the conversation lagged since I knew nothing about Nyack, New York.

I tried again.

"Before you went to Cornell what did you do?"

"What everybody does. Went to school, high school, college, worked in the summers."

He seemed determined to be uninteresting and untalkative. I said: "Is that all?"

"After college, four years in the navy."

That seemed to open a door.

"On a ship? Where did you sail?"

"In a naval ordnance laboratory in Bristol, New Jersey. I was a chemistry major in college. The navy needed chemists. That's where I got started in plastics. They use more plastics than anybody, and kept testing new kinds. For ship fittings, gun covers, frogman suits, even hulls. Plastics that wouldn't chip, freeze, crack, corrode, or leak."

"I see." I saw the conversation steering into a circle.

"And when I finished there, I applied at Cornell Graduate School." End of circle.

It seemed hopeless, and I should have given up, but I did not. Instead I said:

"But were you ever—did you ever—get married?"

He looked at me in a queer way. He said: "I thought you were coming to that."

And then it happened. To my absolute astonishment, he did not even smile, but reached over and took my hand. "Grabbed" would be a better word. He took it very quickly and hard, pulled it to his chair, jerking me toward him so that I almost fell over. He held my hand between both of his.

He said: "No, I never got married. Why did you ask that?"

I was so startled that for a minute I just sat and stared at him. All I could think of at first was that somehow he had misunderstood something I had said.

After that I felt embarrassed, awkward, and afraid, in that order. Embarrassed for a quite unimportant reason—because my hand was hard from working and his were soft, from wearing those plastic gloves so long, I suppose. Awkward because, the way he had pulled me, I could not sit right in my chair, but was leaning off balance. And afraid, finally, because when I tried to pull away he just tightened his grip. There was nothing gentle about the way he held my hand, and no expression at all in his face. He looked at me in the same way as he had looked at *The Farm Mechanic*.

He said again: "Why did you ask that?"

I said: "Please let go."

He said: "Not until you answer."

I said: "I asked because I was interested." I felt myself beginning to tremble. I was really frightened.

He said: "Interested in what?" And instead of letting go, he tightened his grip, pulling me farther off balance.

I could not help what happened next. I felt myself falling from the chair, falling toward him, and quite instinctively I threw my right hand up (he was holding the left one) to catch myself. It hit him in the face, not very hard, on or near his left eye. In that moment he pulled back and relaxed his grip. I snatched my hand away and sprang back.

In a very quiet voice he said: "You should not have done that."

Why should I have apologized? I still don't understand, but that is what I did.

"I'm sorry," I said. "I didn't mean to. I was falling." In my confusion I may even have tried to smile; I cannot remember clearly. Then I left the porch and went back to the kitchen. As I left he said:

"You held my hand once before."

In the kitchen I was shaking so hard that at first I could not continue the cooking; I could not think clearly. I thought I was even going to cry, something I seldom do, but I managed to hold back. I sat on the kitchen stool and tried to calm down. I told myself it was not really so important. It was the kind of thing the girls at school used to tell about after they had had a date. But it happened when they were on their way home to their parents. It's different when there's no one to turn to or tell about it. And I found myself doing what I have long since banned myself from doing—that is, imagining my parents were coming back, with David and Joseph, and wishing they were. I put the thought out of my head, as I have learned to do. But I felt somewhat calmer, and was able to continue with the dinner.

He walked back to the bedroom by himself. I was still cooking when I heard the sound of his cane and the dragging thump of his feet; he was holding himself up by leaning against the wall. Eventually I heard the bed creak as he reached it, and when I carried in his food, he was sitting there surrounded by his diagrams. He took the tray calmly, as if nothing had happened. I ate in my usual place at the card table, but we did not talk.

It was true what he had said about my holding his hand. On the night when he was sickest, when his pulse was almost gone and his breathing only a flutter, when I thought he was dying, I sat by his side and held his hand. I am not sure how long; I think several hours. I had not thought he would remember it; as with the music and the reading I was simply trying to let him know that I was still there.

What he had done was not the same at all. There is a telepathy that goes with such things. When he was holding my hand, I could tell that he was taking charge, or possession—I do not know how to put it. He was trying to control me, just as he had, in his way, controlled the planting, the use of the gasoline, the tractor, and even my going to church. And, of course, the suit, and, in the end, Edward.

For that reason his walking back to the bed without help, which should have been something to celebrate, instead makes me uneasy.

SEVENTEEN

June 30

I am living in the cave again, and I am glad now that I never told Mr. Loomis about it or where it was. I moved up here two days ago, not because I wanted to, but because of what happened. I will try to write it down in order. That may help me to think clearly and decide what I must do.

On the night after the hand-holding, I went to bed as usual with Faro beside me. I was still extremely nervous and could not get to sleep until about 3:00 A.M. When I woke it was bright daylight—later than usual for me—and I had the worried feeling that everything had changed. At first I could not think why; then I remembered, and again I tried to convince myself that it was not so important. I had my work to do and I ought to do it as before.

So I got up, gathered the eggs (noting that one of the hens had hatched out eight baby chicks—all alive!— and two others were setting), milked the cow, went into the kitchen, and got breakfast ready. And it *was* all as before except for my own feelings. I ate breakfast in the kitchen—I had been doing that each morning, since he did not wake as early as I did—and then, after cleaning things up a bit, took his tray into his room. I felt strained and tense, but if he had any such feeling, he did not show it at all. He took his tray, started eating his breakfast, and, as usual, we talked about what I would do that day. I had planned to fertilize the corn and the soybeans, which were now up. Also the garden if there was time.

He asked: "Fertilize with what?"

"The corn and beans with chemical fertilizer."

"From the store."

"Yes."

"How much is there?"

"I don't know exactly." The fertilizer, in fifty-pound bags, was kept in a shed behind the store, next to a loading platform. The shed was full, the bags stacked to the ceiling. Mr. Klein had been ready for the spring planting by the Amish. "There must be 500 bags."

"Still it will run out."

"But not for years."

"It must last until we can switch to manure."

"I know."

I felt better down in the cornfield, driving the tractor and the spreader through the rows of new corn. It was doing well, several inches high already, the young stalks shining bright green and looking healthy. I tried to imitate my father and get the wheel—and thus the fertilizer—as close to the rows as I could without packing them down. The day was bright and still; in fact, for the first time it was a bit warmer than comfortable in the sun, and Faro, after following me for a couple of rows, went to the edge of the field and watched from the shade of the apple tree. All in all, I felt normalcy returning and then, turning at the end of a row, I glanced up at the house. There on the porch sat Mr. Loomis in his chair, leaning slightly forward. Because he was in the shade, I could not see his face, but I could feel that he was watching me.

That made me feel nervous again; I could not tell exactly why. I tried to overcome it by not looking in his direction again, not even a glance, but pretending (mostly to myself) that I did not know he was there. I concentrated on the rows, and watched the spreader and the gray fertilizer sifting down from the hopper onto the soil. When I turned off the tractor at noon and walked up to the house, he had gone in again.

Lunch was about as usual, and then I went out again.

In the late afternoon I fertilized the vegetable garden, this time using manure. I hauled it in the old wooden handcart, some from the pile outside the barn, some from the henhouse. I used manure not because of anything Mr. Loomis had said but because we always did; it makes the garden grow better than the chemical fertilizer.

All in all it was a fairly routine day until dinner time, and even what happened then was not really startling.

It was 6:30. I was in the kitchen and had almost finished cooking. In fact, I was putting knives and forks on the tray when I heard the sound of his cane and the thump of his footsteps (somewhat brisker than before) coming out of the bedroom. I thought he must be going to the porch; I listened, standing quiet, and instead heard him turn in the opposite direction—toward the back of the house, toward me. I thought: is he coming to the kitchen? I heard a chair scrape, a thump, and when I looked out he had seated himself at the dining room table. He saw me in the doorway.

"I don't need to eat in bed anymore," he said. "I am still weak, but not sick."

I put away the tray and set the table instead. We ate together, he at one end of the table, I at the other. He even tried to create conversation.

"I saw you driving the tractor. I was on the porch."

I said: "Oh?"

"Was it hot in the sun?"

"A little. Not very."

"Some tractors have sunshades for the driver."

"You can buy them. My father never did. He liked to work in the sun. When it got too strong he wore a straw hat."

There was a pause; we ate in silence. Then he said:

"I thought the corn looked good." He was paying me a compliment.

I said: "It's okay. So are the beans."

"And the vegetable garden."

We were, in fact, eating spinach from the garden for dinner, and in a few more days would have peas.

He kept this up, a sort of inconsequential chatter, and I joined in as well as I could. I even told him about the eight new chickens. And I did feel a little more relaxed as a result, which I suppose was what he had intended.

After dinner I washed the dishes as usual and swept the floor. I was yawning, feeling quite tired. When I came out of the kitchen I saw that he had not gone back to the bedroom. He had decided that he was no longer sick, so he was sitting in a chair in the living room. He had even lighted two lamps, though it was not really dark out.

He said: "Do you remember when I was sick—something you did?"

I was immediately alarmed, thinking he was coming back to the hand-holding.

"What do you mean?"

167

"You read to me. At least once, for quite a long time."

I was relieved. I did not mind discussing reading. "I remember."

"Could you do it again?"

"You mean now?"

"Yes."

"Read what?" I was not very eager to do it, partly because I was tired, and partly because it seemed strange and unnatural. Why should he want me to read to him when he knew how to read himself? Still, I knew of families who did read to one another as a regular pastime; perhaps it was not so strange.

"Whatever you like," he said. "Maybe what you read before?"

"That was poetry."

"I don't mind. I'd like to hear it. Or anything else you want to read."

I did not *want* to read anything, but the fact is I did not know how to refuse.

So I ended up reading to him for more than an hour. I read Gray's "Elegy" again, and when I finished that he asked me not to stop, so I read the beginning of *Pride and Prejudice* by Jane Austen.

After the first half hour or so I realized that he was not listening at all. I discovered this while reading Jane Austen. I was so tired by that time that I accidentally turned two pages at once, skipping from page seventeen to page twenty. I read on for half a page before I realized that I had left out the whole episode telling about Mr. Bonaventure and his money, so that what I was reading made no sense. I started to explain and go back to page eighteen when it came to me that he had not even noticed. So I just read on.

But why should he ask me to read to him if he did not want to listen? I was puzzled and worried.

The more I thought about it, the more the feeling grew in me that it was wrong; it was as if he were playing some kind of a trick on me. And that idea made me feel more nervous than ever—in fact, afraid. Then I got quite angry with myself for feeling that way. I told myself I was making up problems. There was no reason to believe that he did not really want to be read to, even though he did not pay close attention. The sound of a voice can be soothing; surely he must be bored and restless with inactivity. I reminded myself that that, at least, was sure to get better as he was able to walk farther and do more. I must be patient.

EIGHTEEN

Still June 30

That was my self-lecture, but it did not work perfectly. I continued to feel uneasy; in fact the next night was slightly worse. He asked me to play the piano.

Again he was sitting in the living room in my father's chair, with two lamps lit. Playing the piano should have been, in a way, better than reading, since I was reasonably sure that he would at least listen—I knew he had liked it before. The difficulties were mechanical and (again) I thought, probably not really important. First, I was tired, and piano playing is harder than reading. Second, I had to sit with my back to him, and I felt unreasonably wary about that.

Did I expect that he would come creeping up on me from behind? I did not really think he would, and yet as I played the first piece, a Clementi Sonatina, I had a terrible urge to look over my shoulder. I kept trying to play softly so I could hear if he moved. As a result I played very badly, hitting more wrong notes than right ones. I resolved to do better on the next one, so I picked a very slow and easy *Andante* by Heller (from the *Easy Pieces*), one I knew almost by memory, and I concentrated on it. It was quite long; I did the repeats, and it was going well—when all at once I heard his cane tapping behind me. It tapped twice, clearly and sharply, and I could not control myself. I whirled around on the bench. He was still sitting in the chair.

He said: "Is something wrong?"

"Your cane," I said. "It startled me. I thought—" I stopped, not wanting to say what I had thought.

"My cane slipped," he said, "but I caught it."

I turned and tried to play again, but my hands were shaking so badly I could not really do it. His cane had not looked as if it had slipped. It was hooked over the arm of his chair and his hand was resting on it. I was really nervous. I tried a hymn, but halfway through it I had to stop.

"I'm sorry," I said. "I can't play anymore. I guess I'm just too tired."

"Tired so soon?" he said.

171

"I've been working all day," I said. "I suppose that's why." Of course that was not why at all, and I was pretty sure he knew it. I thought he had tapped the cane purposely, just to see what I would do. But why should he?

He said: "There is too much work. But quite soon now I will be able to do some of it. Then you must show me how to operate the tractor."

It was a reasonable suggestion, but when I went to bed, it kept me from sleeping. It was ironic; as a child I hadn't particularly liked working in the fields. I had preferred to cook or feed the animals. Yet now I felt best when I was out there alone, working in the garden or running the tractor.

The next night he did not ask me either to read or play the piano. I was a little surprised, since dinner was over a bit earlier than usual, but I decided it must be because the night before I had said I was tired. In fact, after dinner he did not sit in my father's chair at all but disappeared into his room.

So, since it was still light after I had cleaned up the kitchen, and the evening was pleasant, I went with Faro for a walk. There was no breath of wind; everything was quiet; it was the time of the long twilight that valleys have while the sun is still setting outside. We walked slowly down the road to the church, and I felt glad and almost peaceful again at being away from the house. Faro seemed to feel the same way—at least he did not scurry around and sniff, but just plodded along quietly, his toenails clicking on the blacktop. When we reached the church, I did not go in, but sat on the edge of the small white porch outside the front door; Faro lay on the step and rested his chin on my feet as he sometimes does. Up above in the belfry I could hear the two crows in their nest clucking themselves down for the night; I could also hear the higher twittering of at least two or three babies, one of which I had found behind the altar.

When they had quieted down and the air was turning gray, I stood up and started back to the house. At this time of evening, at this season, in the old days, the whippoorwills would fly in and we would hear them singing in the pine trees, sometimes so loudly they kept us awake. But now all I heard was a beetle buzzing past; up the hillside I saw a few fireflies blinking, the first I had seen this year. I was glad there were some of them left, at least.

About halfway back, the house came into view, rather vague in the dim light. I was even with the pond and was just looking to see if there were any fish-ripples on the surface when a movement straight ahead caught my eye. I stopped and looked harder. It was Mr. Loomis walking from the house to the wagon; it reminded me of the time before, when he was so sick and had fired the gun. But he walked more purposefully this time, and so far as I could see, he was not even using the cane.

I could not see exactly what he was doing, but he walked slowly around the wagon, bent over it a couple of times, and then stood up straight and stared down the road. I did not think he could see me, since I had stepped a way off the blacktop to look at the pond; Faro was sitting still in the high grass. After about two minutes (I stayed still) he turned and walked back to the house, mounting the porch steps carefully, holding onto the rail. I suppose he had been checking on the safe-suit. He definitely did not have the cane.

I waited until he went back into the house and the door closed behind him; then I started to walk back, but for some reason, did not want to quite yet. So I sat down on a hummock beside the road and watched the fireflies some more. Finally, after about half an hour, when it was fully dark, I went back. The house was unlighted. I went directly up to my bedroom and sat on the bed. Faro came in with me, lay down, and went to sleep immediately.

I lit a candle, set and wound the clock, and sat for a few minutes thinking what I must do tomorrow. I felt sleepy after my walk but uneasy. I kicked off my shoes but decided not to undress, at least for a while.

The next thing I knew, I woke up in pitch darkness; the candle had burned out, and Faro was growling. The growl changed to a short *yip* of surprise; his feet scuffled on the floor, and he ran out. I wondered what had

174

startled him and then, in the next second, I knew. Mr. Loomis was in the room.

I could not see anything at all, but I could hear his breathing. I knew in the same second that he could hear mine. I started to hold my breath but realized that was foolish—he knew I was there. So I tried to breathe normally; I tried not to tremble, hoping he would think I was still asleep, and perhaps go away. He moved, very slowly and quietly—he *did* think I was still asleep. But I was never more wide awake.

He crept forward until he was right beside me, just where Faro had been. I felt his hand, groping, touch the edge of the bed. Then, suddenly, both his hands were over me, not roughly, but in a dreadful, possessive way that I had never felt or imagined. His breathing grew faster and louder. He was not going to go away. I could sense that, and I knew what he was planning to do as clearly as if he had told me. One hand brushed my face, and then came down hard on my shoulder to pin me to the bed. At that instant, pretense ended. I whirled to one side, sprang to the floor, and made a dive for the door. In the same second his whole weight landed on the bed where I had just been.

But I had tripped over his leg in my dive and before I could get my balance his hand, grabbing blindly, had caught my ankle. His grip was strong; I was amazed at his strength. He was pulling me back, and my hands, grasping for something to hold, slid backward over the smooth floor. His other hand groped forward and caught the back of my shirt. I pulled forward again, heard the shirt rip and felt his fingernails tearing the skin of my back. I hit back with my elbow as hard as I could.

By good luck I think I hit him in the throat. He gave a gasp, and his loud breathing stopped momentarily. So did his grip on my ankle and shirt, and in a burst I was out the door and running, my shirt rent down my back.

NINETEEN

June 30, continued

I did not sleep anymore that night. After I got out of the house, I ran, not thinking where I went, not caring. I just wanted to get away as fast as I could. As it happened I ran down the road toward the store and the church. I could not hear that he was following me, but I could not be sure, because my ears were pounding with my own heartbeats. I ran at top speed for, I think, a minute or more. Then I slowed down enough to look over my shoulder. Although there was no moon that night, it was clear, the sky was bright and I could see the road plainly. There was no sign of him. I had slowed to a dogtrot as I passed the pond, and when I reached the store I stopped, got partly behind it, and sat down where I could still watch the road.

I did not think he could run, but I could not be sure—I had also not thought he could walk without the cane.

I sat for an hour or more, getting my breath, trying to stop shaking. Faro was nowhere to be seen, but I knew where he was. He had hidden under the porch. He always did that. When there was any friction between people—if my father or mother had had to scold Joseph, David, or me for instance—he would sense it and hide. He had heard the struggle, of course. If he had not, if he had not been there in the room to wake me up in time, I do not know how it would have ended.

After a while I felt thirsty and very cold; a small, chill wind had blown up, and I thought of the blankets that were still in the cave. I could pull one on over my torn shirt; I could sit at the entrance and keep watch. At that point my brain began working again, at least a little, and I remembered that I had no shoes and no other shirt at the cave—I had taken my clothes back to the house—so while I was at the store I had better get new ones. I would need them because I knew I might never go back to the house again, at least not as long as he was there.

It was coal black inside the store, but I knew the shelf where Mr. Klein kept the matches, and also where he kept the candles. I groped my way around and got a

178

candle lit. In the clothing section of the store—it is on the rear right as you come in—I picked out a pair of sneakers my size and two shirts, one cotton, one flannel. I put on the shoes and flannel shirt (being so cold) and was just buttoning it when I heard a *thud* up near the front of the store. I jumped so hard I knocked the candle over, and it went out.

I should not have been so frightened, I know. But I was. I started shaking again, and just stood there in the dark listening. There was no other sound. Then I thought: the door! That was what had happened. I had left the door in the front of the store open about six inches, and the wind had blown it shut. I relit the candle, my hands shaking so I could hardly strike the match, and went to the front. It was the door—that was all. Still I wanted to get out of there. I was not used to being such a coward.

Outside I felt better, and walked, carrying my extra shirt (and the candle, which I blew out and put in my pocket) to the pond. There, where the brook flows in, I drunk and rested. Except for the water and the blinking of the stars there was no movement anywhere. Yet I felt in danger.

I walked on. In the cave—I had not been there for weeks—I could see by candlelight all was as I had left it. I put a blanket around my shoulders and sat in the entrance, in my usual place, where I could lean back against the rock wall and look down on the house. In the dark it was visible only as part of a blur that formed the yard, the trees, and the bushes. There was no light in any window that I could see.

I sat there all the rest of the night, watching. I was sure he did not know where I was, or where the cave was, or even that there was a cave. I did not think he could climb the hillside. But I watched anyway.

In the early morning the scene below slowly took shape and color. The leaves turned light gray and then green. The house turned white, the road black, and the hilltop behind me grew bright. I got my binoculars from inside the cave. It seemed important to observe what, if anything, he was going to do. I had a feeling he would be really anxious to know where I was.

The first movement was Faro, coming hesitantly around the corner of the house, sniffing as he came. He circled the house, went to the tent, circled that, and then set off down the road, his nose still to the ground. He was following me.

Within ten seconds of this Mr. Loomis appeared. He must have been watching out the front window. He walked to the edge of the road, limping a little—but without the cane—and stared after the dog. He went a few feet, then stood on the road a minute, thinking. Finally he walked back to the house. I could guess a couple of things from that: he had not seen or heard which way I ran, but he knew that Faro would follow me. That was why he had been watching.

It was lucky that in my confusion I had run down the road and not straight up to the cave. I knew what Faro would do. He would track me to the store, from the store back to the pond, and from the pond to where I sat; but Mr. Loomis could not see that from the house. I could almost time Faro's movements. Sure enough, in about ten minutes he came up through the woods, wagging his tail.

I patted him and was glad to see him, but that was all I did—I was still intent on watching the scene below. Faro stayed with me for about ten minutes and then, after sniffing around inside the cave, he trotted off down the hill, back to the house. I had been feeding him in the morning; it was time for his breakfast and his food dish was in the yard near the front porch. I suppose he thought I would follow him.

I realized then that I should have fed him at the cave. I did have a few cans of meat—three to be exact—and also some canned hash that he would have eaten in a pinch. But it did not occur to me until after he left. And I began to realize that Faro could—quite innocently—lead Mr. Loomis to me and that if I had fed him and kept him with me, I might have prevented that.

A few minutes after Faro reappeared in the front yard Mr. Loomis came out the front door, carrying his dish, full of food. He put it down, and as Faro began to eat, I could see that Mr. Loomis had something else in his hand. Through the binoculars it looked like a belt, and that is what it was—one of David's or Joseph's, I suppose. He had cut it off short, and as Faro ate he slipped it around the dog's neck and fastened the buckle.

Faro did not seem to mind much; he gave a shake or two and then went back to his eating. Mr. Loomis meanwhile went to the porch and got something else. At first I thought it was a piece of rope but then, from its bright green color, I knew it was not. It was a long electric cord, the one from my mother's vacuum cleaner. He slipped it through the belt around Faro's neck and knotted it. He tied the other end to the porch rail.

Poor Faro! He had never in his life been tied up. When he finished eating, he shook himself again, trying to get the collar off, and then trotted away. When he came to the end of the tether, his head snapped back and he fell down. He stood up, shook himself, and tried again. Next he turned around and backed off, trying to pull the collar over his head. Mr. Loomis watched; at last, having seen that the dog could not get away, he turned and went back into the house.

Faro, following the instinct of all dogs, sat down and chewed on the cord. But it was made of heavy wire with a tough plastic coating, and though he kept gnawing for half an hour, it was too much for his teeth.

After that he cried, a thin mournful yipping sound he had not made since he was a puppy. I wanted to run down and untie the knot, but of course I couldn't.

So I sat where I was and watched. Also, I began to think about what I should do, what was going to happen. I thought about all the routine things I should be doing—milking the cow, feeding the chickens, collecting the eggs, and weeding the garden. Could I just live up here, keeping my distance, and continue to do my chores? Perhaps the outdoor things I could. Cooking the meals I could not do, since that would mean going into the house. Mr. Loomis would have to cook for himself. Should I continue to bring him supplies from the store? I did not think he could walk far enough to get his own, not yet. I could not let him starve, no matter what he had done.

I decided that somehow or other we would have to work out a compromise, a way that we could both live in the valley even though not as friends. There was enough room, and he was welcome to have the house. Perhaps I could live in the store or church. I was willing to do the work as necessary. And we could stay apart, and leave each other entirely alone.

The trouble was, though I would be willing to do that, I was not sure he would be.

Still the effort had to be made. I decided I would go and talk to him, keeping at a distance. I was thinking of how and what to say when I fell asleep.

I woke up in the late afternoon. My neck was sore and stiff, and I was hungry. I had only a smattering of food supplies, but I opened the can of hash and ate it cold.

My next job is to figure out where I can build a fire, either by day so he will not see the smoke, or by night so that he will not see the flame. I expect the second way will be easier.

TWENTY

July 1

After supper, in the cave.

Mr. Loomis does plan to use Faro to catch me. Yesterday, late in the afternoon, he came outside carrying a plate of food. The dog had stopped crying and gone to sleep, curled up in the grass beside the porch. Mr Loomis did not give him the food immediately, but put the plate down on the porch. He untied the leash, the electric cord, from the porch, looped up most of it in his hand like a lasso (it was twenty-five feet long), and led Faro out to the road.

Faro, not used to being led, had a hard time at first—he kept trying to run and each time was brought up short. He learned quickly, however, and in a few minutes was walking along docilely enough, his nose to the road. He was following my trail again, but this time leading Mr. Loomis behind him.

They went only a few yards up the road together, perhaps fifty. Then they turned and went back to the house, Mr. Loomis once again limping slightly. But in that few yards I began to see even more clearly the mistake I had made, and also why Mr. Loomis had tied Faro up. If he could teach him to track on a leash, he could find me whenever he wanted to. Not yet, perhaps, but when he could walk farther.

Suddenly I had a feeling he knew I was watching. Or worse, that he hoped I was. I felt slightly sick; I was in a game of move-countermove, like a chess game, a game I did not want to be in at all. Only Mr. Loomis wanted to be in it, and only he could win it.

After he had tied the dog up and fed him, Mr. Loomis walked back to the road and stood looking in the direction they had walked, toward the store. Having seen nothing there, he turned slowly in a full circle, inspecting all of the valley that he could see. At one point he stared straight at me, and I had a fearful impulse to put down the binoculars and duck into the cave. But he could not see me, I knew; in a moment his gaze went on past, he completed his circle, and went into the house.

I took stock of what I had in the cave: a few pounds of cornmeal in a paper bag, some salt, three cans of meat, three of beans, one of peas, two of corn. That was all the food—not very much. I had the two guns and a box of shells for each. A sleeping bag, a pillow, and two blankets—but no change of clothes except for the extra shirt I had brought from the store; the rest I had taken back to the house. A pot, a frying pan, a plate, a cup, a knife, fork, and spoon. Two candles, a lamp, and a gallon of kerosene. One book, *Famous Short Stories of England and America*, which we had used as a textbook in high-school English. And three bottles of water—former cider jugs, holding one gallon each. However, the water had been in the cave for weeks and might be stale. After dark I would pour it out and refill the bottles at the brook.

The sun was going down, and I decided before it was fully dark I must see about making the fire. What I had in mind was to build, if I could, a wall of some kind near the cave, not very big, but enough to hide the glow of a small fire from the direction of the house.

It turned out to be quite easy. I found a more or less flat place, a shelf, on the hillside a few yards up. I dug into it with a stick, raking the loosened earth with my hands into a low pile on the downhill side. The resulting hole was about six inches deep, about the size of a wash-basin, big enough for a cooking fire. The pile of earth was too low to hide all the flames, so until dark I collected rocks, about brick-sized, for my wall. When I had enough, or nearly, I found I could no longer see well enough to fit them properly; so I decided to finish the next day, by daylight, and ate cold beans for supper.

After I had eaten, I carried two of my bottles to the brook and refilled them with fresh water. I also rinsed my spoon and washed my hands and face. I felt very tired in spite of my nap; I was yawning continuously and realized there would be no staying awake that night. That alarmed me somewhat because sound asleep at night I was vulnerable. I decided as a precaution not to sleep in the cave—with its one entrance, and that a small one, it would be like a trap.

I took my sleeping bag and a blanket up to the shelf where I had been building the fire wall. There was just room enough on the other side of the hole to stretch out. The ground was lumpy, but it made no difference. I fell asleep instantly and did not wake up until the sunlight reached my eyes this morning.

I got up, washed, ate (the rest of last night's beans), took my bedding back to the cave, and set out for the house. I went the long way around, of course, by the pond and the store so that I could approach along the road as I had left. I did not want him to have any idea where I was staying.

Approaching the house I saw no sign of life or motion. The tent stood in the yard, and the wagon-trunk beside it sealed in its green cover. Where was Faro? I thought he would be tied outside, but he was not. When I came up to the front yard, I stopped, staying in the road, and waited. I planned to go no closer than that.

I did not have long to wait. In only a minute the door opened and Mr. Loomis stepped out onto the porch. He had seen me from inside. He came down the steps, and stopped at the bottom.

"I thought you would come back," he said. Then he added, "I hoped you would."

For a moment I was stunned and could not think what to say. He was sorry and wanted to be friends again. Yet I could not forget the horror of that night, and I knew that I would never trust him again.

"No," I said, "I am not coming back. Not anymore. But I thought we should talk."

"Not come back?" he said. "But why not? Where will you stay?"

It was as before, the time he had held my hand and I had struck him. He acted as if nothing had happened, or as if he had forgotten it. For a moment I thought, maybe, somehow, he did forget the things he had done. But I knew it was not true; he had not forgotten. He was, rather, pretending that it had not happened.

I said: "I will find someplace to stay."

"But where? This is your house."

"I would rather not discuss it."

He shrugged, very unconcerned. "All right. Then why did you come?"

"Because although I can't stay here anymore, I need to stay alive, and so do you."

"True," he said. "I intend to stay alive." He was looking at me curiously, thinking as he talked and not necessarily saying what he was thinking.

"If we are to stay alive," I said, "there is work that has to be done. There are the crops and the seeds, the garden, the animals."

He said: "Of course that's why I thought you would come back."

"I'm willing to do those things if I am left alone. I will also bring food and water as you need them. You will have to cook for yourself. There is a cookbook on the kitchen shelf."

"And you will go away at night. Where?"

"To another part of the valley."

He was thinking all the time. He glanced down the road in the direction of the store. Finally he said:

"I have no choice. I can only hope you will change your mind," he paused, "and act more like an adult and less like a schoolgirl."

"I will not change my mind."

He said no more, but turned and went back into the house, closing the door behind him. I went to the barn, trying as I went to guess what he was thinking. He would be making plans, and from our conversation he had learned some things he had not known and needed to know: that I was not going to move back to the house, that I was going to do the work; that I was going to bring him food and water. So he would plan on that basis. But plan what? It is possible that he will just accept what I have offered, and leave me alone.

But I do not believe that. He was too curious about where I am staying. And he has tied up Faro. Where was Faro when we talked? There was no sight nor sound of him. He must have had him tied up inside the house. Does he think, then, that I might try to untie him—to steal him? (As Edward stole the suit.) As I remembered that I did, in fact, think of doing that, I had a really sickening thought. I realized that whatever Mr. Loomis was planning, at the end of the plan was a picture, and it was of me, too, tied up like Faro in the house.

I put the idea out of my mind and milked the cow. She was going dry; there was no doubting that. The calf was almost fully weaned, and I had missed several milkings in a row, which had helped to speed the process up. Though I was careful to get the last drop, she gave only about half a gallon. There were assorted milk pails hanging on the barn wall; I poured the milk into two of these, dividing it evenly, and put one of them on the back porch for Mr. Loomis. I fed the chickens, gathered the eggs, and divided them, too, four apiece. From the garden I got peas, lettuce, and spinach, took half and set the rest on the porch. Finally I got a burlap feed sack from the barn to put my stuff in, though it barely filled one corner.

In short, I did my morning outdoor work about as usual, and he left me alone, not even coming out onto the back porch. I did have a feeling he was watching me through the kitchen window, though I caught no glimpse of his face.

About noon I went to the store to get him a load of groceries. I ate lunch there, from a can on the shelf, opening it with one of the can openers Mr. Klein had sold for forty-nine cents. When I carried the groceries back and left them on the porch, there was smoke coming from the chimney, and the milk, eggs, and vegetables were gone. He was cooking lunch. I made a mental note of two things: if I was going to continue to bring groceries, he would have to let me know what he needed; if I was going to bring water, he would have to set one of the water cans out when it got empty.

At four o'clock, having run the cultivator between the rows of corn and beans, I quit and walked back to the store, thinking as I went that for one day, at least, the system had worked. It was unnatural and uneasy, but if it worked again tomorrow, the next day, and the day after that, perhaps I would become less afraid. So my hopes were lifted a little. I also thought that if I could get the wall finished, I could build a fire after dark and cook a hot meal. I was quite hungry.

I stopped at the store to replenish my food supply. Since I had my burlap feed sack already with me, I used it as a container, removing the four eggs first. I gathered a dozen cans of assorted meats, vegetables and soup and a bag of flour. I put the eggs in a brown paper bag and added them on top. With the garden stuff I already had, that was about all I could carry, since I had to keep one hand free for the milk can. I decided to take a few more items each day, gradually building up my supply.

I deposited my foodstuffs at the cave and hurried on, while it was still light, to finish my fire wall. The more I looked at the site I had chosen, the better I liked it. For one thing there were plenty of bushes and quite a few trees between it and the house; in fact, I could not see the house at all from there, so I was quite sure that with a little care I could keep the fire quite invisible. I added more rocks, chinking them with dirt and moss. In about half an hour I had a respectable-looking small fireplace, its back about eighteen inches high on the downhill side. Since my fire would be built in a six-inch hole, flames under two feet would not show. That seemed enough. I gathered some dry sticks for firewood.

While waiting for darkness, I looked down on the house. Mr. Loomis had come out again with Faro on the leash and was walking with him, this time not down the road as before but out behind the house. At first I did not understand just what his object was, but as I watched, it slowly became clear.

When they had walked before on the road, Faro obviously tracking, Mr. Loomis had guessed he was following me. Now he was making sure.

I got out the binoculars to see better. As soon as they got behind the house, Faro put his nose to the ground and led the way to the garden—where I had been. Then to the barn—where I had also been. Faro, in other words, knows what is expected, and Mr. Loomis, having watched from the window all day, knows that he knows.

Finally Faro led him to the last place I had been before leaving, the barn where I had put the tractor away after cultivating. Here Mr. Loomis stopped. He opened the door, looked in, and then, seemingly as an afterthought, looped Faro's leash around the door handle. He disappeared into the barn.

He was out of my sight, but it quickly became apparent what he was doing. After perhaps five minutes, I heard the churning metallic sound of the starter, and the sputtering of the engine, muffled because it was inside the barn. A minute later it grew louder, and the rear wheels of the tractor appeared, moving cautiously as he backed it out.

He had, as far as I knew, never driven a tractor before—hence the five minutes. That was what it would take to figure it out for anyone who knew how to drive a car. The clutch, gas, and brake pedals were the same; the gearshift similar, two speeds forward and one reverse, plainly marked "1," "2," and "R." Even the ignition key and steering wheel were the same.

Mr. Loomis backed the tractor all the way out of the barn, shifted into forward and drove it in a small circle in the barn lot. He shifted into neutral and raced the motor a little, as if to hear how it sounded. In forward again, he drove it back into the barn and turned it off.

He untied Faro from the door; the dog picked up my track again and started to lead the way toward the store. But Mr. Loomis, already knowing I had gone that way, led him back to the house. It was growing dark. A few minutes later I saw a light come on in the kitchen window. If he was cooking, there must be smoke coming from the chimney. In the dusk it did not show, and I thought, if I could not see his, he could not see mine. I had laid my fire; now I lit it, got it going—small but enough to cook over—and crept carefully through the bushes halfway down the hill toward the house.

There I waited until the dusk had turned to full darkness, looking alternately at the house (to see if he came out to look) and up the hill toward my fire. The wall was successful; there was no trace at all of flame or glow. The only danger might be an occasional spark; I would have to be careful about that. I went back up the hill and in a few minutes was cooking myself a dinner of canned ham, cornmeal cakes, peas, and scrambled eggs. I was extremely hungry.

After I had eaten I felt tired and, though I should have gone to the stream to wash my dishes, I began to write in this journal.

I wish now Mr. Loomis had never come to the valley at all. It was lonely with no one here, but it was better than this. I do not wish him dead, but I wish that by

195

luck, by chance, he might have taken some other road and found some other valley. And I wonder: Could there be others? Walking here from his laboratory, he came south; he went no farther than this. Could it be that somewhere beyond there are more valleys like this, other places that have been spared? Perhaps bigger than this, with two, three, or half a dozen people still alive. Or maybe no people at all. If Mr. Loomis had taken another road, he might have found one of them.

It *is* possible. My parents explored only a small area. There might be, for all I know, another valley only a few miles away, or even several. They would all be isolated from each other, each thinking it was alone.

When Faro returned that day, I was astonished and puzzled about where he had been. Could he have been living in another valley? Could he have run to it from this one and then run back? There is no way of knowing. I do not even know which direction he came from when he returned.

TWENTY-ONE

August 4 (I think)

I am in terrible trouble. I haven't written in my journal for several weeks. I have been too sick and too afraid. And I've had to keep moving. I am hiding now in thick woods high up on the west ridge near the gap at the south end of the valley. There is a hollow tree where I can keep my things and when it rains I get in the tree, too. It is all a nightmare. What happened is Mr. Loomis *shot* me!

For about ten days we had a sort of system. I would go down in the morning and milk, get the eggs, feed the chickens, work the garden, pick the vegetables. Each day I divided the food evenly, and left his share on the back porch. When he needed drinking water, he set out a can and I filled it at the brook. I brought groceries from the store; twice he came to the back door as I was leaving the eggs and asked for specific things—he had run out of salt; he needed cooking oil. The rest of the time I used my own judgment, and he accepted what I brought.

There were inconveniences. I missed the kitchen, the stove, the laundry tubs. I looked at the ripening tomatoes and wondered how I was ever going to can them; I decided it could be done over an outdoor fire, perhaps near the barn so I could use my father's workbench as shelf space for the jars, of which there were plenty in the store. I worried, too—ridiculously, I know—about the condition of the house, whether he swept the floors, and even about how he did his laundry, if indeed he did it. My own, such as it was, I did in the brook.

At sunset, after the second milking, I would go back to the cave, always by way of the road and the store. Once or twice I stopped off at the church, but that, like keeping up my notebook, I tended to neglect. It seemed strained. I do not know exactly why. Churches, I suppose, must be associated with normalcy. I did pray some, but only at odd times during the day. The Bible was out of reach in the house.

I saw little of Mr. Loomis except from a distance. He seemed to have given up and accepted the new order of things; and yet I was almost sure he had not. Still, I lived—what else could I do?—as if it were going to continue this way. I even began to worry about the winter, about cutting firewood.

Each evening he would come out of the house just before dark, almost always with Faro. They would walk, and practice tracking, going a little farther (and Mr. Loomis a little more briskly) each time. After the first few days, he began trying a new method: he would let Faro off the leash but keep him close, either by talking to him or whistling softly, I could not hear which. Faro had always recognized the command "Close," but in the past only when there was a gun along.

Three or four more times he took the tractor out again. Once, toward the end of this period, he took it on a longer ride than just around the barn. He drove it up across the yard toward the house, and then out the road. There, heading right, toward Burden Hill, he shifted it into high gear and revved the motor up. He ran it at top speed for about three hundred yards—he was obviously trying to see how fast it would go, though I did not know why. It can make about fifteen or eighteen miles an hour—quite fast enough when you have no windshield and no springs.

On the morning of the tenth day (or, as I said, it may have been the twelfth or even fourteenth), I got up, ate breakfast, and took my things to the cave. I looked down at the house just in time to see something new.

Mr. Loomis came out the door, walked quickly to the road, and then, looking definitely furtive, started toward the store. He did not stay on the blacktop but went along the edge, the side toward Burden Creek, walking where there were trees and bushes to hide him.

I got out the binoculars to see if I could tell what he was up to. As he walked he stared straight ahead, up the road toward the store, as if he were looking for something. But looking for what? Then I realized—for me, of course. He wanted to see me when I first appeared, to see where I was coming from.

He stopped, finally, at a clump of trees where the road made a slight bend. From that point he could see the store itself in the distance.

That meant that if I took my usual route, he would see me approaching the store from the pond, and would know at least which side of the valley I was living on. And I thought: why let him know that? Yet I did want to go down as usual, get my eggs and milk and do my work.

The answer was simple enough: I used another approach. Staying up on the hillside, near the top of the ridge, I worked my way to the far end of the valley, almost to the gap and the steep cliff on the far side. On the way I passed just above the crab-apple tree where I had once picked a bouquet; looking down on it, I could see the young green apples hanging thickly on the branches.

I came down to the road far beyond his range of vision—I could not even see the store. I crossed the road and headed back, keeping to the trees that bordered the creek. They gave way to brush, and then the store came in sight.

I walked carefully so as to keep it between me and the spot where he was watching. And when finally I reached it, I stepped quickly out from behind it and onto the road. I wanted to make it look as if I had appeared from nowhere. At least he would have no clue as to what direction I had come from.

I went on toward the house. As I came to the trees where I had seen him I had another thought: suppose he was not just watching. Suppose he tried to catch me. I approached cautiously, ready to turn and run—but he was not there, and when I came in sight of the house I saw him on the porch just going in the front door. So he had retreated when I came in sight, none the wiser for spying.

I went about my work as usual. When I had gathered the eggs, I took them to the back porch and saw that he had set out the milk pail and also one of the water cans. The milk pail reminded me that in my concern over choosing a new route, I had forgotten to bring my own pail, and also to bring anything to carry my eggs in. So I gave him all of the milk; two of the eggs I left in the hen house, thinking I would pick them up when I left and carry them back in my hand. And tomorrow, I would remember to bring both sack and pail.

Another small problem: a brood hen had hatched out six more chicks. That meant there were now fourteen babies coming on—and two more hens were setting. Under such circumstances I would ordinarily feel justified in having one of the older hens for dinner—but how could I clean it? Where and with what? I could not go into the kitchen. My only knife, except my pocketknife, was in the cave.

There was an obvious solution to both problems. I took his water can and set out for the pond, carrying it in full view so that if he was watching from the window he would see I was merely going to get him some water.

At the pond, out of his sight, I put down the can and ran up the hill, staying safely in the woods on the far side of the stream. I got the knife and also, while I was there, picked up the milk pail. I was back filling the water can in four or five minutes, somewhat out of breath. At the house I deposited his can of water on the porch beside his milk and eggs, confident that I had escaped suspicion. As it turned out, I was wrong.

I cleaned the hen in the barn on my father's workbench, cut it up into frying-size pieces, and divided it evenly into two piles, one for him, one for me. Being a rather old hen it would have been better roasted, but I could not help that; he would find it edible if a bit tough.

Having deposited his half of the chicken with the other food, I went to the garden to hoe around the tomato plants. They were now, with the benefit of the manure, growing tall and leafy and showing hard little green tomatoes. I decided to stake them. The stakes were in the tack room of the barn, as was the tying-twine, so when I finished hoeing I tied them up. There were twenty-eight plants in all. If I could solve the canning problem, there would be enough stewed tomatoes to last all winter. It seemed ironic, having finally gotten myself a stove, not to be able to use it.

I would give him half and store the other half in the cave, where it would not freeze. I thought about all this as I ate my lunch (two cornmeal cakes from my pocket); I sat leaning against the garden fence, and when I had finished I rested awhile, admiring the potato plants, which looked healthy, with leaves of a lustrous dark green. Potatoes, too, would keep well in the cave. After resting, I got up and went to the barn to get the tractor.

And then my serious trouble began, for though the tractor was in its usual place the ignition key was gone.

I searched on the floor, my first thought being that Mr. Loomis, after he had used the tractor last night, had accidentally dropped it. The floor was of wide, heavy planks, almost black in color and unlittered, so that if the key were there it would have been instantly visible. It was not.

I remembered something. We had always left the key in the tractor, and to make sure it did not get lost my father had tied it loosely to the steering column with a piece of wire: one forgets things like that when they are always there. So Mr. Loomis could not have dropped it accidentally. He must have taken it with him, and quite deliberately, since it would have required time and effort to unfasten the wire. But why? All I could think of was that in his desire to conserve gasoline, he wanted me to ask him each time I used it, and let him know what for.

There was another ignition key; I even knew where it was kept, but it did me no good. It was on my father's key chain, in his pocket somewhere out in the deadness.

I decided: there was nothing for it; I would have to go up and ask him for the key. It was, after all, his crop as well as mine that needed cultivating.

I walked to the house, around to the front, and stood in the road as before, in plain view of the windows. There was no response immediately; but there was smoke coming from the chimney, so I guessed he was in the kitchen cooking his chicken. After five minutes of waiting I gathered my nerve, stepped onto the porch, knocked on the door, and quickly retreated. Faro set up a barking inside, and a minute later Mr. Loomis appeared. I suspected he had seen me go to the tractor shed and so knew why I had come, but he pretended not to.

"Back again?" he said, very pleasant. "A surprise! I must thank you for the chicken. I was just frying it. If you would like to come in . . ."

"Thank you," I said. "I've had my lunch."

"Too bad," he said. "Still, you have your half, don't you? But where will you cook it?" He had been wondering where I cooked—no doubt looking for signs of smoke or fire. I ignored the question.

"I came because I couldn't find the key to the tractor."

"The key?" he said, mildly surprised. "Oh, yes. I have driven the tractor a few times, in the evening, just to learn how. Perhaps you knew? And now I have decided to keep the key in the house. It will be safer here."

I said: "But I need it. I was going to cultivate the corn."

He came forward and sat down on the porch steps, as one does to chat with a passing neighbor. I noticed that although he held onto the rail he sat down without any sign of effort. His legs were getting back to normal; the stick had been abandoned.

"I have to think about that," he said. "I have not yet made up my mind." His pleasant manner vanished abruptly. "You see, if you are going to continue this stupidity, this staying away, there are things you are going to have to do without."

"But the corn—"

"For example, the stove. I suppose you should have that, too, after you worked so hard to move it. And there are other things you will miss. More and more as times goes on."

I said: "It was your idea to plant more things, and I

agreed that it was right. Now surely you want them to grow."

"I said I have not made up my mind. I will think about it, but not now. I left the chicken cooking—your cookbook says fifteen minutes on each side. It's time to turn it over." He stood up—again quite easily. "Possibly I will run the cultivator myself."

He walked to the door. As he was going in he said: "It was thoughtful of you to bring your knife along with the milk pail. But then, how else could you have cleaned the chicken?" He shut the door behind him.

I stood there staring after him, feeling bewildered, baffled, and stupid. Baffled because I did not know what to do; bewildered because I could not understand why he would not let me use the tractor. And stupid because from what he said last I knew I had made a thoughtless mistake. After thinking I had been clever—taking his water can to the pond, running to the cave and back—I had returned visibly carrying the knife and the milk can. Of course he had watched me both going and coming, and so knew I had gone to fetch them at wherever I was staying—and that it must be not more than a few minutes from the pond. I was only lucky he could not see the pond from the house; I had not given away the whole show—only half of it.

Mainly I did not know what to do, my plans for the afternoon having been cancelled. I walked to the barn and sat a few minutes, leaning my back against the rear wall, looking out into the pasture and thinking. Why had he taken the key? Did he really intend to do the fertilizing himself? He could, of course; the spreader was simple to operate.

A new thought came to my mind; it seemed very obvious and clear. He had taken the key because he was afraid I would steal the tractor. The more I thought about that, the more I believed it. It was part of a pattern, like the safe-suit, like tying up Faro. He had made plans involving the tractor; therefore it suddenly became valuable; therefore I might not have it.

I had, as it turned out, guessed correctly. And I learned soon enough what he wanted the tractor for.

Meanwhile, having nothing to do, I collected my two eggs, my half chicken, and my knife and walked slowly down the road to the store. My milk can I left at the barn; I would come back at four to milk again and would fill it then.

As I walked, I kept looking back to see if he was following, and when I reached the bend—a little beyond it I stopped and waited to see if he would come back to his grove of trees again. He did not, though I was sure he had watched me out of sight through the window.

There were several things I wanted from the store, and I took this opportunity to gather them up: more clothes, for one thing, so I could wash mine at the brook; some soap, some more canned food. As an afterthought I took some fishhooks and fishing line. Mr. Klein did not sell rods and reels, and mine was in the house, but I could fish well enough without one.

My goods assembled and stowed in a brown bag, I debated whether or not to go directly up the hill to the cave or take the long route. Though he had not appeared at the grove while I waited, he might have come to it since. Eventually I compromised, and walked half a mile in the wrong direction toward the gap, keeping the store between me and his line of sight. Then I turned left, was quickly in the trees, and worked my way back to the cave.

I cut a sapling for a pole, found some worms under a log, and went fishing. I would have chicken for dinner and, with luck, fish for breakfast.

TWENTY-TWO

August 4, continued

By four o'clock I had caught and cleaned three middle-sized fish. From the pond as I sat I could look down on the field of wheat, a darker green acre in the pasture that stretched toward the gap. We were not trying for a real wheat crop, but only a harvest of seeds, and it would surely produce that, at least. I put the fish on a string and walked to the house. I placed his share, one and one-half fish, on the back porch, hoping he was watching so he would know to pick them up. The cow was waiting to be milked and fed, but gave only half a can of milk—less each day, but better than none, which was what it would be soon. I turned her back out to pasture, closed the barn door, put the top on my can and walked back to the store, through for the day.

I had reached it and was debating which way to go when I heard the tractor engine, faint in the distance. It was earlier than he had used it the other times, and I wondered why. It sputtered slowly for a couple of minutes, and then suddenly smoothed out and was running fast. It got louder very quickly. He was on the blacktop, and was coming my way at top speed.

I debated no longer, but made a dash up the hill, to the right of the pond, to reach the woods behind it before he turned the bend. I slopped a bit of my milk, but I made it. Once in the woods I circled to the left as I ran to reach a spot from which I could watch. I did not worry about crashing noisily through the brush: the tractor engine was getting louder all the time. I found a vantage point behind a bush, set down my milk, crouched, and waited.

The tractor had come out of the trees and ran in plain view down the blacktop, covering the last half mile to the store. Mr. Loomis sat astride, steering with his left hand. In his right, to my amazement and horror, he held his rifle. He looked like an Indian on horseback in an old Western movie, attacking a wagon train. I stared, at first not comprehending at all.

About a hundred feet from the store he turned the tractor halfway around and stopped it, leaving the engine idling. He climbed down on the far side, keeping it between him and the building. He stood there watching for a minute or two, then cut the engine and put the key in his pocket. Holding the gun in both hands, he moved toward the store. His eyes were on the windows and the door.

I remembered how he had acted once before, when he fired two shots into the house. He's suffered a relapse, I thought; he *is* back in his delirium. But no, it was quite clearly different. That time he had been dreaming. There was nothing dreamlike in the way he moved forward now, alert as a cat, to the door. He paused, listened, and backed away. He looked to the right, to the left, behind him; then moving more quickly, he circled the building, disappearing from my view, reappearing, staring at every window, upstairs and down. Back at the door, he opened it with the greatest caution, then pushed it wide and stepped inside.

I stayed motionless behind my bush, watched, and wondered. Why was he storming the store? "Storm" was the word I thought of, because that was really how it looked—like a surprise attack. Why the gun? Did he intend to shoot something? To shoot me? Why else does one carry a gun?

For ten minutes or so all was quiet. I stared at the building and the tractor. A movement caught my eye—a curtain pushed aside in an upstairs window, and his face looking out, pale in the dark frame like a ghost in a haunted house. And I knew part of the answer.

He was not in the store proper at all. He had gone up to the Kleins' living quarters on the second floor. He was, of course, looking for me.

I had deceived him too well. Each night when I left the house I had walked toward the store. In the morning, when he had watched, I had appeared suddenly beside the store. That same morning I had gone to get his water from the pond—in the same general direction as the store—and reappeared carrying things of mine, milk can and knife. So he had, quite sensibly, decided that I was living in the store. He had, I supposed, the first time he went into it, discovered there were living quarters upstairs—perhaps he had even gone up and looked.

But, in fact, I had only been in the Kleins' apartment one time since they drove away that day with my parents. It was on a rainy Sunday, after I had been to the church. Since it was Sunday I did not want to work; it was too rainy to fish or to take a walk as I sometimes did, and by then the radio stations had all gone off. So I had decided to read, and as always, was wishing I had some new books. It occurred to me the Kleins might have had some.

Their apartment was shadowy, too heavily curtained for a gray day. It was entirely clean, as Mrs. Klein—a small and tidy woman—would have left it, but it had a stale smell from being shut up. I felt quite uneasy, though I had been there once or twice before; it was a private place, and everything in it belonged to two dead people. I knew as soon as I entered I was not likely to find any books, and there were none—not even magazines—with two exceptions: a dress pattern book near Mrs. Klein's sewing machine, and some account and inventory books in a room Mr. Klein used for an office.

I even looked in their bedroom, feeling guiltier than ever, but there was only the usual furniture and some pictures on the walls. Also, the only thing in the whole apartment that was out of place. It was a photograph of a young man, smiling, dressed in a dark suit and necktie, in a stand-up frame. It looked quite old. It lay on the bed face up. I wondered who he could be. Either Mr. or Mrs. Klein had obviously looked at it one more time before leaving. A son? I could not recall anything about their having a son. It might have looked a little like Mrs. Klein when she was younger, so perhaps it was a brother. I never found out, of course. I left it lying on the bed.

The point was, however, that Mr. Loomis was sure to know at a glance that I was not living there. That was why he had looked out the window. If I was not there, he was thinking, I must be somewhere in the vicinity.

He came out the front door again, looked around, and went back in. When he reappeared about thirty seconds later from behind the store—he had walked straight through it and gone out the back door, which I could not see from my vantage point—he had left the gun inside. He walked a few yards away, turned, and appeared to be studying the building, tapping his chin with his hand. Then he disappeared again—I could guess he had gone in through the back door—and for fifteen minutes or so I could not see him.

I thought of the gun again. It was frightening to see. But perhaps not so frightening as it had seemed at first. I was beginning to get used to the way his mind worked, the way he thought about things. There was a pattern that kept repeating. In the case of the gun it meant—or, I thought, it *might* mean—not that he was planning to shoot me, but that he thought I might shoot him. I still think that might be correct. He may have reasoned that if I was encamped in the store and saw him coming, I might be frightened, and might try to drive him away. But what made him think I had a gun at all? My guns had been at the cave all of the time since his arrival, and I was quite sure I had never mentioned them.

He had had plenty of time for thinking, I realized. And during the past two weeks he must have recalled his first day here, the day he came over the hill in his safe-suit pulling his wagon, and went to the house. He had seen, thanks to my carefulness, that it was empty and had not recently been lived in. Thinking back on that, he would realize that I had had, even then, another place to live.

He would know, too, that in a country household, where people hunt, there are always guns; so he would assume that if I had moved out of the house, I would have taken them with me. All this he would have thought of, sitting by himself in the house day after day, and of something else as well. He would have decided that if I had a place reasonably comfortable and well set up (not just living in the woods), I was not so likely to give up after a few days and move back to the house—to stop the "stupidity," as he called it—unless he did something to force me to do it.

The sun was getting ready to set when I saw him again. He came around from behind the building; he must have gone out the back door again; and he carried something in his hand. In the waning light, without the binoculars, I could not see what it was; only that it was small and it was not the gun.

He walked to the front door and stood before it. Because he was under the porch roof, in the shadow, it was hard to see just what he was doing. But he seemed to be examining the door itself, and even reached out and touched the frame with his hand. He put down whatever it was he was holding, went inside, and came out again almost immediately, carrying something else. For the next fifteen minutes he stood there working busily, at what I could not see but only guess.

At the end of that time he made one more brief trip into the store and emerged with the gun; he started the tractor and drove off toward the house. When I heard the motor fade in the distance and finally sputter and die,

I stood up and came out from behind my bush, not forgetting my milk and fish. It was getting dark.

I considered going on to the cave, but I was too curious. I wanted to see if what I guessed and feared was right. I walked down to the store to look, and it was. He had put padlocks on both front and back doors, and both were locked.

That night, back at my fireplace, I changed my plans and cooked the fish, which would not keep, and wrapped the chicken, which would keep, in a piece of paper and put it in a cool place in the cave. I was thinking about the padlocks without any keys and the tractor without any key. At first I thought that, to go into the store and to use the tractor, I would have to ask permission each time. But then I had a worse thought:

He was not going to give me any of the keys at all, to anything.

TWENTY-THREE

August 4, continued

It was the next morning he shot me.

I woke at dawn as usual, moved my blanket and sleeping bag to the cave, and ate the rest of the fish for breakfast—cold, but cooked, not so bad. As I ate, I cheered up a little and thought possibly, just possibly, I had been too pessimistic about the padlocks. I knew that he had a compulsion for taking charge of things, for saving things, for rationing them out in an orderly manner so they would last—like the V-belt, the gasoline, the fertilizer, and so on. A long-term view. And he did not trust me to do that (perhaps rightly)—hence the locks. Maybe that was all it meant.

In any case I had to find out, fearful as I was of the answer. Because the other alternative was that he had thought of a simple way to force me to come back. Starvation. I could not help considering that, too. If it was his plan—what would I do? I had food enough in the cave for a couple of weeks, maybe longer if I did not eat much. I could fish. I knew where berries grew. I could possibly shoot a rabbit. But it was obvious that in the long run I could not live.

And what about the chickens, the eggs, the milk, the garden? Would he somehow lock them up, too?

There was little point in wondering. I had to find out.

So, feeling worried and quite depressed, I took my milk can and my sack and walked to the house, going the long way around. It seemed especially important now to keep him from finding where I stayed.

As I walked, I had another thought: perhaps, in a way, these new things he had done were my own fault. It seemed that the more I stayed away from him the more determined he was that I come back. Perhaps I could yield a little. There are people who cannot stand being alone; perhaps he was acting from despair. Why should I not, then, offer to talk to him, if he wanted me to, say for an hour or so in the evenings—he on the porch, I on the road? It could do no harm. There was no reason I should not be as friendly as safety permitted. It was a sensible plan and made me feel better.

When I came in sight of the house, I decided not to go about my work as usual, but to let him know straightaway that I had seen the padlocks, and ask for the key. I had to get it settled. It was, in fact, time to bring him some more stores anyway. And at the same time I could suggest my new idea.

I know now that he was watching as I came up the road and was expecting me to come to the house. Not that it made any great difference in his plans when I came. I would have had to ask eventually.

I remember now that my father once said that great events have a way of happening uneventfully. They slip up on you and are over before you know they have happened. This could hardly be called a great event, I suppose, but it was for me an important and terrible one, and it happened almost without my knowing it.

I stood there in front of the house as I had before, watching the front door, thinking I would go and knock if he did not appear. There was a sharp snapping noise. I was wondering what and where it could be when I felt a hard tug on the leg of my blue jeans and a sting of pain in my right ankle. The noise came again. Not until then did I look up and see the shiny blue rifle barrel, very thin, the upstairs window six inches open and his face behind it, partially hidden by the curtain.

The second shot missed, hit the blacktop a foot behind me and flew away humming like a bee.

I dropped my milk can and ran for my life; the can hit

the road with a clang and rolled away. Faro, in the house, hearing the shots and the clanging, barked in a frenzy. I dashed for the trees beside Burden Creek, expecting each second another bullet to come crashing into me—because for the next thirty yards my back was still a clear target. But he fired no more. I even thought I heard the window shut, but did not pause to look.

In the trees I felt reasonably safe; I made my way, dodging from tree to tree on the far side of the road. At the bend, where I could look back and see that he was not following, I sat down to examine my ankle. The bullet had gone through the leg of my blue jeans, leaving two small round holes, and the sock underneath showed a narrow, straight tear through which blood was slowly oozing. I removed my sneaker and sock. Below was a small, shallow cut, barely through the skin, bordered on both sides by a white area, very sore to touch, which was going to be a bruise and turn black-and-blue.

As wounds go, it was not serious; in fact while I sat there looking the bleeding virtually stopped. Still it brought to mind a lack in my supplies: I had no bandage, no disinfectant of any kind. There was some in the house, some in the store, both now out of reach. Then I remembered. I did have soap at the cave. I could wash the cut, at least, and put on a clean sock. I tied my shoe on loosely and walked on.

As I washed my ankle I thought it was a most peculiar wound, and puzzling. He had fired two shots. If he was trying to hit me, both had been aimed much too low. He might just be a very bad shot, but that hardly seemed likely. Not with me standing stock-still (for the first shot, at least) and him in a prepared position, waiting, with the windowsill for support—nobody could be that bad a shot. Was he trying to miss? Trying to scare me away? Maybe. And yet, in a way, that made him even a worse shot. Anyone, shooting, can miss when trying to hit something. But to hit when trying to miss it—

And then, sickeningly, the truth came to me.

The idea, the scene, the things that happened in the next minutes, the next hour, were so bad that I do not like to think about them. Each time they come back to me, they are like a nightmare and I am living them over again.

I was sitting beside the pond with my sock in my hand and my shoe beside me, waiting for my foot to dry. The piece of soap was on a stone at the edge of the water. And I suddenly realized that he was not trying to miss. He wanted to shoot me in the leg so I could not walk. He wanted to maim, not to kill me. So that he could catch me. It was a simple plan, a terrible one. Starvation would force me to come to the house or the store. And the gun would keep me from going away again. And I knew he would try until he succeeded.

Why? That was all I could ask.

As I sat there by the pond, I heard the tractor start. I knew by some instinct before I saw it what was going to happen next. So I put on my sock and my shoe as fast as I could and ran up the hill to the bushes where I had hid before.

The tractor, looking bright red in the morning sun, came out of the trees. On it, as before, holding his gun in his hand, rode Mr. Loomis. The gun barrel shone like a tube of blue glass; it was the small rifle, the .22; he did not want to shatter my leg, only cripple it, because after I was caught he intended it to mend again.

The tractor came out and behind it was hitched the tractor-cart. In the tractor-cart, tied by his leash, sat Faro. He was enjoying the ride. He had always liked to ride in the cart.

Mr. Loomis stopped at the store as before, climbed down, gun ready. That time he knew I was not inside, but he also knew I had more reason to shoot if I was hiding nearby. So he looked about him sharply. Then he took Faro down from the cart, and began the game they had practiced. Holding the leash, he circled the store. Faro picked up my trail immediately—the freshest one, leading toward the house. Mr. Loomis did not want that one.

He tried again, a wider circle, and that time it worked. Faro started retracing my morning's route, tail wagging, backtracking easily. And suddenly that small friendly dog, David's dog, was an enemy, as dangerous as a tiger, because I knew what he was going to do. He would lead Mr. Loomis a mile down the road; he would turn left and lead him up the hill and to the cave.

The nightmare lasted an hour. That is how long it took Mr. Loomis, who did not hurry (but did not limp either), to make the trip. Long before that I had run to the cave. My time there was up. I knew it was. I had my cloth sack, the feed bag I had brought from the barn, and I threw into it what I could carry, not choosing very well because I was, stupidly, crying and because my ankle was hurting badly. I took cans of food, this notebook, a blanket, my knife, some water. That was all I could manage, that and a gun. I took the small rifle, the pump-action .22, and put a box of shells in my pocket.

I had no place to go except higher up the hill and into the woods. I chose a spot overlooking the way they had to pass as they approached the cave. There, waiting, ready to run again, I had the worst part of my nightmare. Because I suddenly saw what I must do. Wherever I ran, as long as Mr. Loomis had Faro, he would find me. I knew that, therefore I had to shoot Faro.

I loaded the gun, found a hummock for a gun-rest, and lay behind it. Fifteen minutes later I saw branches moving; they were still a quarter-mile down the valley, still on my trail. My ankle ached worse than before, but the crying had stopped; I felt sick to my stomach but my eyes were clear.

At last they were directly below me. Mr. Loomis was going very slowly and limping a little; Faro was tugging at his short leash. In clear view Mr. Loomis stopped to listen and I had a stationary target. I drew the bead, the gun was steady and I could not miss. But at that moment Faro gave a small, impatient tug and a small bark, which came clearly up the hill to my ears. It was his bark of greeting, a soft pleasure bark for me—he knew the cave was just ahead. And at the sound, so gentle and familiar, my finger went limp on the trigger, and I could not do it. In the end I lowered the gun barrel and they moved on out of sight.

In a few more minutes they were at the cave. I could not see them from where I was hidden, and I did not dare go closer because I knew he would be watching.

I smelled smoke, retreated farther up the hill and looked back. From the direction of the cave I saw it: a thick column, rising fast, as if it came from a bonfire. Feeling sicker—quite dizzy in fact—I sat down and loosened my shoe.

For half an hour the smoke continued; toward the end it grew thinner and finally faded away. Then, in the distance, I heard the sound of the tractor engine. It grew fainter as it moved toward the house. Mr. Loomis had walked enough for the day and was going home. When the sound had stopped, I knew it was safe, and I made my way, sparing my right foot, back to the cave.

It was hard to keep from crying again. In front of the entrance in a black and smoldering pile were the remains of all my things. My sleeping bag, my clothes, even the box I used as a table and the board I had for a bench, all were cinders. My fire wall had been kicked down and scattered. My water bottles smashed. I saw in the heap a part of the charred cover of *Famous Short Stories of England and America*. The few cans of food I had left he had taken away—at least I saw no signs of them in the fire. And the other gun was gone. Inside the cave I found one thing he missed. My half-chicken was still in its cranny.

That was, and is, my nightmare. The worst part of it was that I really did decide to kill Faro. I am glad I could not pull the trigger, but that does not alter the fact. It makes me feel as much a murderer as Mr. Loomis. Now there are two of us in the valley.

And in the end I did kill Faro, though not with the gun.

TWENTY-FOUR

August 6

It is raining, and I am sitting in the hollow tree to keep dry. I slept here most of last night—after the rain started. It is cramped, and I worry about spiders. Even so, I feel more hopeful than I have in a long time. My ankle is almost well, but the main reason I feel hopeful is that at last I have decided what to do. I have made a plan: *I will steal the safe-suit and leave the valley.* The idea came to me while I was sick.

For several days after I was shot, I was aware of very little. I think I had a fever, though I had no thermometer to find out, and my ankle swelled very large and looked bad—blue on one side and bright red on the other. I did not attempt to walk on it—it hurt too much when I put it down. When I had to move, I hopped on one foot. But most of the time I lay still, wrapped in my blanket. I slept a great deal.

Sometimes I thought I heard noises in the distance—the sound of the tractor running, the sound of hammering—but I could not be sure. Mr. Loomis, if he had known it, could have tracked me down easily with Faro's help and caught me, because I could not run. But of course he did not know it, since the injury had seemed slight, and when he last saw me I was sprinting at high speed. He must have assumed that he had missed. So he was busying himself with other things assuming I would have to come out eventually—and he missed his chance.

It was during those days of sleeping that a dream began, a dream I have had many times since. At first the dream was not very clear to me. I was only aware of the sense that I had been walking in a strange place, and of a feeling of disappointment when I awoke, at finding myself still in the valley.

People's dreams bore me generally; before this one I have had only a few that I remembered longer than a few seconds after I awoke. Yet this dream was more important than any I had ever heard of before or dreamed. Coming night after night, it began to dominate my thoughts, so that first I hoped and now I believe in what it seems to tell: there is another place where I can live. And I am needed there. There is a schoolroom lined with books, and children sitting at the desks. There is no one to teach them, so they cannot read. They sit waiting, watching the door. When I am sleeping I can see their faces, and I wish I knew their names. They look as if they have been waiting for a long time.

And so I have decided to leave the valley. I am convinced, since the shooting incident, that Mr. Loomis is insane. We will never be able to live in the same place in peace. I have lived in constant fear of being seen and hunted down: the sound of pebbles sliding on the rocks, a twig snapping, even the wind in the leaves can make my blood run cold. The valley, which has been home and shelter for my whole life, seems now to threaten me wherever I go, whatever I do.

At first my plan was very vague, really not much more than a wish. I would think of the place in the dream and wonder where it was. From what I could remember, it was not so different from places I had visited as a child; not north, because my parents and Mr. Loomis had seen the deadness in the north, but maybe south or west. There are many valleys to the south and west, all with farms, a store, a school. Was it so unrealistic to think of people there, alive, afraid to leave?

I decided to go to them. I would prepare myself for a long journey and a long search. I would go as Mr.

Loomis had before me—wearing the safe-suit, pulling the cart. I would take the binoculars, and perhaps the gun. I would walk as far as I could each day, looking for the children in the dream.

Once I had developed the plan, and had begun to realize that it was not just a wish but something that I was actually going to do, there were many things to think about. I had no idea how much food remained in the wagon, and of course I would also need water. I didn't know how the air tank worked, or whether I could adjust the safe-suit to fit me. Most important, I had to figure out a way to get the suit and cart without being seen, and shot. One person, Edward, had already lost his life because of the suit, and I knew that Mr. Loomis would not hesitate to kill me for it if necessary.

For almost a month now he has left me alone. I do not know why, but I know what he has been doing, because every morning I can hear the tractor engine starting, and it continues, sometimes loud, sometimes quiet until mid-afternoon. Several times I have hidden behind the brush farther down the ridge and watched. He will be cultivating the garden or hauling in wood for the winter. Always he seems intent on what he is doing, so that I almost feel as if I could sneak down the hillside into the hen house to gather eggs, or fish in the pond without his noticing. But of course the risk is too great.

How have I lived? When I explain, it will seem strange that I did not choose to leave long before now, for my life during this time has been more miserable than I ever thought possible. Much of the time I have been hungry. I have picked mushrooms and blackberries on the ridge; for anything else, I have had to sneak into the valley at night. I have stolen vegetables from the garden I planted myself, and eaten them raw, or cooked them over a fire at night. Sometimes when there's been no moon or the sky has been cloudy, I have fished at the pond. That has always been frightening, for I have always felt that he would guess I might come, and wait there to trap me. Once I sneaked into the hen house and took eggs, but the chickens were scared, thinking from my approach at night that I was a weasel or a fox. They crowed and squawked until I was sure that he would hear them in the house. I have never gone back.

Even worse than hunger has been the monotony of my days. In daylight I can not go anywhere without the fear of being seen and shot at, so mostly I have stayed hidden at this end of the valley. I have slept quite a lot, for it is cool and shady here even during the hottest days. I have worried, of course, that Mr. Loomis might use Faro to lead him to my new hiding place and trap me here while I was sleeping. But the drone of the tractor has been reassuring.

Sometimes when I've been sitting in the woods, waiting for dark to fall so that I can go out safely, I have thought about my book. I've remembered the stories that were my favorites, and sometimes I've even been able to remember the exact words an author wrote in some special scene. But I've also remembered how I found the book that night when I went back to the cave after he had burned my things. That memory stirs my harshest feelings toward Mr. Loomis. I am not sure I have ever hated anyone—as a child I was taught that hatred was wrong—yet I admit that I want to hurt him, and cause him grief. He deliberately ruined the thing I prized most. Stealing the safe-suit will be my revenge.

I have thought about the plan a lot. Still, as miserable as my life has been, I was not able to bring myself to set the plan in motion, or even to make the first move for a long time. I suppose it was fear that held me back, and the fact that, for the moment, Mr. Loomis was leaving me alone. Yet it has always been only a question of time: fall will come, and my food sources will be gone; and Mr. Loomis will not wait forever.

As it was, it was he who set the plan in motion, without knowing what he was doing, and without my knowing it either. On a warm afternoon I had grown bored and decided, against my better judgment, to go to the east ridge of the valley to gather berries. They were plentiful and delicious and I ate almost as many as I picked, stooping behind the bushes to keep out of sight. At one point I glanced downward over the farm and seemed to notice something different, but my eyes came back to the blackberry bush, and it was not until I looked a second time that I realized what it was. The front door to the store was wide open.

I could not believe my eyes. At first I thought that Mr. Loomis must be inside the store, gathering supplies for himself. I shrank lower behind the brush and waited for him to emerge. I waited for a long time, but there was no sign of him. Then suddenly it occurred to me that the open door might have been an accident. Suppose he meant to lock it and forgot? The longer I waited, the more I became convinced that it was true. He had gone into the store before lunch to get some things he needed, and in his hurry he had forgotten to fasten the padlock. The heavy door had swung open. He had gone down the road to the house without looking back.

I was beside myself with excitement. My mind flooded quickly with the tastes and smells of food I had not eaten for the past month: canned meat, beans, crackers, soup, cookies. I thought of supplies that I needed for the trip: more clothes, a better knife, flashlight batteries, a compass. I would not get another chance to go into the store; I had to take the risk now. Warily I began to creep forward, always staying behind the brush. In the valley nothing moved.

Finally I came to a place where the brush stopped, so there was nothing for me to hide behind. The field, with the pond, stretched to my right; ahead of me lay the road and the store. I walked slowly along the fence row, turning to look on every side. All was quiet. I felt braver and braver. I was only fifty yards from the road, when suddenly a rabbit exploded from underneath my feet and I leaped backward in surprise and fear. Something moved in the window of the store and a shot rang out. I turned and ran. He fired again, but the shot missed widely, and I thought I heard him curse. Faro barked. I made it up the hill into the trees and hid.

I had walked into a trap. I was too shaken to consider my own foolishness; it was only the rabbit, and Mr. Loomis's impatience, that had saved me. But it was not over yet, for no sooner had I gotten into the trees than he was out of the store, the gun under one arm and Faro on the leash. He crossed the road into the field, and Faro found my trail almost immediately. He began to whine and bark. I turned and ran through the woods toward the west ridge. I knew what I had to do.

I ran to the hollow tree and got my gun, then doubled back along my own trail and moved north, crawling through thick brush and saplings. I could hear Faro's barking on the hill below me, but I knew that it would be a time before he would catch up with me; there were many scents to sort through, and my trail was winding. After a short while the brush thinned, and I ran through the woods until I reached the banks of Burden Creek. I had spent many hours there fishing for brook trout with David and Joseph; and although there were no fish left since the war, I remembered the course of the stream bed. I walked partway across the water on a series of flat stones, then jumped across a narrow pool onto a smooth, shallow ridge of rock that connected with the opposite bank. I hurried across the ridge and through more trees, and hid behind a stone. I could see the crossing place clearly, though I was some distance away. I balanced the gun across my knee, and sighted it.

I did not wait long. I was too far away to hear them crashing through the brush, so their sudden appearance near the stream's edge almost caught me off guard. Faro was straining on the leash and was in the water almost before Mr. Loomis knew what was happening. Then suddenly he remembered, and jerked back on the leash. At that moment I aimed the gun above his head and fired.

He had not known I had a gun, and I think he really could not believe it when he heard the shot. He stood still for about ten seconds, then he yelled and leaped to one side. He released Faro and ran into a grove of trees. I fired again, but he had disappeared from sight, and I guessed from the motion of the brush that he had headed downhill, back toward the house.

Faro was swimming in Burden Creek. He had found my scent but, instead of following my trail on the rocks, he had plunged into the water. It was over his head, and he had to fight the current. All in all he was probably in the stream for more than five minutes. Then he found the ridge where I had walked and jumped onto it, and onto the other bank. In a few more minutes he was by my side.

I hid behind the stone until dark. By then I was sure that Mr. Loomis would have left the hillside and gone into the house, so I felt safe in leading Faro to my camp. There I fed him some dried mushrooms and offered him my own dinner of vegetables, but he was not much interested. He slept beside me all night and was sick in the morning. I expected he would be sick for several days—I remembered the course of illness in Mr. Loomis —but I guess dogs react differently from human beings, for by nightfall he was dead.

Now I am ready. I will put my plan into action before daybreak tomorrow morning. It may be that I will not write in this journal again. I know that if Mr. Loomis catches me with the safe-suit, he will shoot to kill.

It is sad when I think how happy I felt when I was plowing the field.

TWENTY-FIVE

August 7

I am writing this at the top of Burden Hill. I am
wearing the safe-suit. I have already taken the cart and
my supplies out of the valley down the road toward
Ogdentown. I have come back for one last confronta-
tion with Mr. Loomis. I must talk to him. I cannot just
walk away from him, from this valley, from all that I
had hoped for, without a word. I know there is danger
in this. He will come searching for me and he will have a
gun; but I have a gun too, and from where I sit, hidden
at the edge of the deadness, I can see the whole valley
spread out before me. I will see him before he sees me. I

will make him stop and drop his gun.

And if he refuses—I try not to think. I know I could not kill him. I will try to run into the brush before he can shoot, to hide in the deadness where he cannot come to search.

While I wait for him, I will finish my account of what happened to me in this valley.

I could not bury Faro; I had no shovel, I carried his body to the east ridge, laid it on the ground, and covered it with stones. I knew then that I could not stay in the valley any longer. I was too sad and angry and did not want to think of Mr. Loomis or see him again.

Last night I slept in the valley for the last time. I lay awake for a long time, thinking of the plan and the dangers involved in putting it into action. I knew that the risks were grave, but there was no reason to wait any longer. In setting the trap for Faro, I had exposed an important secret: I had a gun and bullets. Mr. Loomis could not ignore that. He would be afraid to work outdoors, and would do nothing until he had thought of a scheme to catch me, or at least to get the gun. He would be very careful, and more dangerous than ever before.

Yet there was one thing that was on my side. I remember when I was a little girl, on Sunday afternoons my father and I would sit at the kitchen table playing chess. Usually my father won; he had been playing the game for many years and had the benefit of experience. But there were a few times when I mounted an attack in such a way that every move my father made was in his own defense, so that he did not have time to effect any organized plan against me. My father called this "taking the offensive," and he said it was the way to win. It seemed to me that in my relationship with Mr. Loomis I had finally reached the point where I could "take the offensive." I had caught him off guard and frightened him. I had to take advantage of that.

I slept restlessly and woke several hours before dawn. I got up quickly and ate, then reviewed the order of events to come. There was no time to waste in fear or doubt. I gathered the few things I would take with me—an extra shirt, the flashlight, a knife, my notebook and pencil—and put them in the burlap sack. I added a bottle for water; once I had stolen the wagon there would be no time to stop at the pond, but I knew there was a device inside the wagon that would purify water from radioactive streams and wells. I put in the remaining box of bullets, the binoculars, and a little packet of dried berries and mushrooms I had picked. Finally I picked up the sack, and with the gun under my arm, I left my camp. It was dark on the ridge, and I did not look back.

I walked along the ridge and through the woods. The sky was filled with stars and the moon was full and lighted the tops of the trees ahead of me. I came to a clear space: the floor of the valley was thick with darkness, but the pond shone as round and clear as a mirror. It was a kind of beauty that was strange to me, and although I was still in the valley, I began to feel that my journey had begun. I descended from the hill.

At the pond I filled the water bottle. I would have to drink sparingly; the water would have to last until I came to another stream or creek outside the valley. I came to the road and walked north. My load was heavy now: the sack, the gun, the filled bottle; and it was hard to see in the dark. I followed the road to the top of Burden Hill. There I hid my things in the ravine beside the road and covered them with brush. After marking the spot with an upright branch, I turned and followed the road back the way I had come.

I knew that there were many ways in which the plan could fail. There was a chance that Mr. Loomis would see my approach from the window and shoot at me; I would have to be closer to the house than I had been since the day I was wounded. He might see through the ruse and refuse to leave the house. He might pretend to go and then turn back, and catch me in the act of stealing the cart and suit. He would surely kill me then. I was frightened, but I forced myself to keep walking.

I came in sight of the house. It was only a dark square in the half-light; there were no lights on, and to a casual traveler on the road, no sign of life.

I left the road and circled around the back. With a bit

of looking I found a heavy, round stone under the walnut tree, and then took a folded paper from my pocket. I had worked for hours on the note, choosing my words, rehearsing the message. Now those words were barely visible. I slipped along the side of the house and onto the front porch, where I unfolded the note and laid it in front of the door, setting the rock on top to hold it down. Sure that there was no way he could miss it, I retreated to a hiding place near the creek.

The note said this:

> I AM TIRED OF HIDING. IF YOU WILL COME TO THE SOUTH END OF THE VALLEY, I WILL MEET YOU AT THE FLAT ROCK WHERE THE ROAD CURVES. WE WILL TALK. COME ON FOOT. LEAVE YOUR GUN ON THE FRONT PORCH. I WILL BE WATCHING YOU—I WILL NOT HARM AN UN-ARMED MAN.

Lying in the tall grass under the willows, I watched the sun rise. The sky above the hills turned gray, and the stars faded out slowly, one by one. The land began to resume its daytime shape and color. The sky in the east turned orange, and then the sun appeared above the ridge. Tomorrow I will watch it from a strange place.

Then, almost before I was ready for it to happen, he was there. The front door opened and he stepped out onto the porch. He looked around him and saw the note almost immediately. He snatched it up and gave a hurried look around, then retreated into the house to read it. He stayed inside the house for quite a while. I lay in the grass with my eyes on the door, trying to imagine what he was thinking. I remembered the first time I had seen him up close, when he was lying sick in the tent. He looked much better now; his face had grown brown from working in the fields, and he looked stronger, yet there was still that tense quality in his face that I had first regarded as poetic, and later as a sign of madness. I had not been so close to him for a long time, and thinking about that made me tremble with fear.

But the plan worked. The next time Mr. Loomis emerged from the house, he had the gun under one arm. Again he looked all around, but this time his gaze was higher and more direct; he knew that I was hiding, watching him, from someplace in the distance. He laid the gun on the porch hesitantly, as if he thought he were making a mistake. Again he looked around. For a moment I thought he was going to call out, but he did not call. He walked to the road and turned left, headed for the south end of the valley.

I was stunned. I knew that I should run and get the cart, but I still could not believe that he was really gone. For almost five minutes I lay still in the grass, trembling. I looked to the south: he was walking fast, and was almost out of sight. I did not think he would turn back. I stood up and began to run.

I ran through the field and across the road to the wagon. It looked smaller than I had remembered, and the rain had caused the paint to warp and peel. I lifted the green plastic covering and looked inside. Everything I needed was there: the safe-suit, the packages of food, the air tank, even the Geiger counters. In a short time my life would depend on them; the wagon, and everything it held, would sustain me in a strange world. I went to the front of the cart, stood between the shafts, and picked them up. They were not as heavy as I had imagined. I pulled forward, and the wheels rolled easily over the thick grass of the yard and onto the blacktop.

I passed the house. Visions moved behind my eyes, and I saw the house as I had seen it as a child: climbing the front steps on the way to supper; sitting on the porch at night, watching the fireflies; my grandfather rocking me on the swing; sitting there listening to someone singing, or a phonograph; later sitting on the swing at night weaving long, romantic dreams about my life to come. I felt the weight of the cart behind me and walked on.

As I walked up the road, the wheels of the wagon made a dry hissing sound on the asphalt. A breeze moved the grass and leaves; sand blew against my face. With each step I seemed to move further away from my own life, as it had been; yet everything I saw tied me closer to the valley. I passed the remnants of an old treehouse. What had I hoped for as a child? I strained to remember; but it seemed to me that nothing in my childhood had prepared me for this.

I turned and looked behind me. The road was still. I wondered where Mr. Loomis was, if he were still waiting by the rock for me to come. I imagined his fury when he discovered that the cart was missing, that he had been tricked. I was nervous, so that it was hard for me to turn around and walk on. I tried to think of the dream: the schoolhouse, the faces of the children; but it was hard to fix the vision in my mind.

I was walking toward the deadness. The creek flowed past the roadside, coming from outside, crossing, perhaps, paths that I would follow. The water was as clear as it had always been, and the sound of the stream moving on the rocks was beautiful to me. Yet everything it touched was dead. I thought of Faro and tears came to my eyes.

I thought again of Mr. Loomis. Soon I would see him for the last time. There was a chance that I could leave without seeing him at all. I wanted to do that; yet there was something inside me that resisted the idea. It pulled against me like a weight, like the burden of the cart as I climbed the hill. I remembered his face when he was sick, and my sadness when I thought that he would die. The cow lowed in the pasture below me, as if she knew that I was leaving, or thought I was already gone.

And if I saw him, what would I say then? He would be mad with rage, and ready to kill. He would do anything to keep me from leaving. He would say anything. He would tell me of the horrors of the deadness, of the loneliness of silent roads and fields. He would speak of bodies in the houses and in cars; he would say he *knew* there was no other place: surely he had searched long enough. He would say, Come back to the house, come back, come back: this time I will leave you to yourself.

For the last minutes, laboring hard under the cart's weight on the uphill slope, I did not think at all. Trees began to appear beside me, right and left, and then the shadow of woods. I kept my eyes down. The road curved slightly and then leveled out, and there was a patch of dense underbrush to my right. I dropped the shafts, found the place where my supplies were hidden, and uncovered the sack. I put it and the bottle of water inside the wagon, pulled the wagon right to the border of the deadness. There I took the safe-suit and put it on, and strapped the airtank on my back, after I was sure I knew how it worked. Then I rolled the cart quickly downhill, leaving it on the way to Ogdentown. I came back with this notebook, and the gun.

The sun is high over the east ridge now and the valley is beautiful in the morning light. I do not know what has happened to Mr. Loomis, or where he is; but I will wait for him. He is bound to come, and I must speak to him. His may be the last human voice that I will ever hear.

Mr. Loomis is coming. I can see him on the tractor. I am glad to have told my story.

TWENTY-SIX

August 8

From the start the interview did not go as I had planned. Mr. Loomis came on the tractor at top speed, with the gun across his lap. I shouted to him to *Stop*, to *Halt*; but he did not even slow the tractor. Instead, he came on. I thought perhaps he could not hear me over the sound of the engine, and in desperation I fired my rifle into the air; but if he heard the shot, he ignored it. He drove the tractor to the very top of Burden Hill, just opposite my hiding place. He jumped down and began to scan the road toward Ogdentown.

My heart was pounding and I did not know what to

do. His back was toward me, but I could not shoot him. I was not even sure I could speak, but I tried and my voice came out reasonably firm.

"Drop your gun," I said.

Instantly he whirled and fired in the direction of my voice. He had not yet seen me, but I was no more than twenty-five feet away. I knew it was the end. I was sixteen and I had worked so hard to keep things going and now I was going to die. A wave of disappointment swept over me, disappointment so bitter it wiped out even my fear. I stood up and faced him, my gun leveled at his chest. But he did not see the gun; instead he saw the safe-suit and began to shout:

"It's *mine*. You know it's mine. Take it off!"

"No," I said. "I won't."

He aimed his gun at me. I stood still, holding mine, knowing I could not shoot. I could not think what to do, so that when words came from my mouth even I was surprised and not conscious of having thought. I realize now they probably saved my life.

"Yes," I said, "you can kill me . . . the way you killed Edward."

He stared at me. Then he shook his head, as if he had heard it wrong, or not heard the words at all. Yet he lowered the gun and stepped back.

"No," he said, "you don't know that . . ." His voice was weak.

"You told me when you were sick," I said. "You told

me how you shot him in the chest. You had to patch the bullet holes in the suit. In this very suit I'm wearing, the one that saved your life."

Now Mr. Loomis turned away from me. For a moment he just stood there; I was not sure, but I thought his shoulders were trembling. After a time he spoke quietly.

"He tried to steal the suit . . . the way you're stealing it now."

"I had no choice," I said. "I didn't want to die, and you wouldn't give me anything. During the winter I would have starved on the hillside. I don't want to live with you hunting me as if I were an animal, and I will never agree to be your prisoner." I felt reassured by my own voice and talked on.

"I'll search for a place where there are other people, people who will welcome me. To stop me, you will have to kill me, too."

"It's wrong," he said, but he knew that I meant it, and his tone was frightened and bewildered. I thought he was going to cry.

"Don't go," he said, "don't leave me. Don't leave me here alone."

I spoke carefully. "If you shoot me, you will really be alone. You searched for months and found no one else. There may not be anyone else; but if I should find people, I will tell them about you, and they may come. In the meantime you have food. You have the tractor and the store. You have the valley."

There was bitterness in my voice. And suddenly, feeling near tears myself, I added, "You didn't even thank me for taking care of you when you were sick."

So my last words were childish.

That was all. I adjusted the mask so that it fit tightly over my face, and cool air from the tank flowed into my mouth. I turned my back on him. I waited for the jar and the sharp pain of a bullet, but it did not come. I went into the deadness. I heard Mr. Loomis calling after me, but the mask covered my ears so that his voice seemed garbled and far away and I could not understand. I walked on. Then suddenly his voice came clearly to me, and I realized he was calling my name. There was something in his tone that made me stop and look back up the hill. He was standing at the edge of the deadness. He was pointing to the West, and he seemed to shout the same thing over and over.

"Birds," he said. "I saw birds . . . west of here . . . circling. They went away, and I couldn't find the place. I saw them."

I raised my hand to him to let him know that I had understood. Then I forced myself to turn and walk away.

Now it is morning. I do not know where I am. I walked all afternoon and almost all night until I was so tired I could not go on. Then I did not bother to put up the tent, just spread my blanket by the roadside and lay down. While I was sleeping the dream came, and in the dream I walked until I found the schoolroom and the children. When I awoke, the sun was high in the sky. A stream was flowing through the brown grass, winding west. The dream was gone, yet I knew which way to go. As I walk, I search the horizon for a trace of green. I am hopeful.